DOCUMENTING **LIGHT**

Other titles by EE Ottoman

DOCUMENTING **LIGHT**

EE OTTOMAN

The Hellum and Neal Series in LGBTQIA+ Literature

Brain Mill Press | Green Bay, Wisconsin

Documenting Light is a work of fiction. Names, places, and incidents either are products of the author's imagination or are used fictitiously. Any resemblance to actual persons, living or dead, or locales is entirely coincidental.

Published in the United States by Brain Mill Press.
Print ISBN 978-1-942083-42-9
EPUB ISBN 978-1-942083-45-0
MOBI ISBN 978-1-942083-43-6
PDF ISBN 978-1-942083-44-3

Cover photograph by Nathan Pearce.
Cover design by Ranita Haanen.

www.brainmillpress.com

For those of us who have gone before.
Your stories will not be forgotten.

CONTENTS

DOCUMENTING LIGHT

CHAPTER 1

T he first thing Wyatt thought when he saw the apartment was that it was beautiful. The ceilings were high, with some orient patterning across each. The doorways in the living room were tall, sweeping arches, and every room had huge windows. There was a built-in bookcase and a fireplace in the living room, with a fireplace in the bedroom as well. The whole place was fresh-painted white walls and gleaming hardwood floors.

"Forget about Mom." Jess turned in a slow circle in the living room. "I want to live here."

"Yeah, if either of us could afford it." Wyatt stuck his hands into his pockets and looked out the living room window at the tree-lined street.

Their mother was a different story. "It's not the farm." She ran her hands over the mantle of the fireplace in the living room, sidestepping the couch the moving men had left jutting into her path. Her big silver hoop bracelets slid and clicked against the wood. "How am I going to walk the dogs without plenty of outside space?"

"You're not bringing the dogs." Wyatt took her hands, turning her gently toward him. "Remember? We talked about this. The Baker boys love them, they'll take good care of them."

"And the farm?" She looked confused, but then they'd expected this. They'd been told the move would be hard and disorienting for her.

"Yeah, they're running the farm now, and you're going to live here, where you can be close to Jess and me."

Timothy, Jess's fiancé, staggered past, his small frame laden with boxes for the kitchen.

"And Timothy," Wyatt added with a pang of guilt. He was glad Timothy was here, even if he would've preferred this to be family only. "It's going to be good."

She still didn't look convinced, though.

"Come on." Wyatt guided her over to one of the built-in bookcases, where boxes of books were already stacked. "Let's get these books unpacked. You know how you want them organized."

He opened one, and for a moment she stared into the box like she'd never seen its contents before. Then her face brightened. "Oh, yes. These are my books on herbal remedies"—she pulled out a handful—"and herb gardening. I see some about wild herb identification in here, too. They'll each need to go together in their own sections."

"Good." Wyatt sat back on his heels as she sorted the books, placing each on the shelf. The doctor had told him that breaking the move into pieces that were manageable for her was the key.

"The rest of these books are on gardening?" She tapped the lid of the next unopened box.

"I'm assuming some of them are." Wyatt ripped the tape off the box and opened it. "But your books on tree husbandry are probably here, too. So each their own section?"

"Oh, I have far too many books on those topics for them to be each their own section. They'll have to be broken down further."

"Then you'll have to do it, and I'll put books where you tell me to, but I don't know this stuff well enough to sort them."

"If you'd paid attention when you were growing up, you would know." But she was smiling, that little teasing smile that said even though she had her mom voice on, she didn't mean it.

It made Wyatt smile back, even as his stomach twisted because he hadn't seen that smile in months and had begun to think he'd never see it again.

It was one of those things you had to let go of. Or at least that's what he'd been telling himself.

"You two look like you're doing good in here."

He turned to see Jess in the doorway looking disheveled in her oldest clothes, curls escaping from the ponytail at the nape of her neck.

"Unpacking?" She smiled encouragingly.

"Yeah." Wyatt waved his arm, taking in the open boxes and bookcase. "We're doing good, organizing the books."

She stuck her hands in her jeans pockets and walked over to look at what they had on the shelf so far. "Well, I think the moving people have gotten everything in."

"I've been organizing by topic. Here, hold this." He thrust a stack of books at Jess.

"You know what, Wyatt?" Jess obediently took the books. "I'll help Mom here for a while if you want to move the boxes in the hall up into the attic. The landlord told us we could use the space up there for storage."

"Sure." Wyatt dusted off the legs of his jeans as he stood and headed into the hall.

Timothy was in the kitchen unpacking boxes of cookware. "You want to order Chinese sometime soon?" Wyatt leaned into the kitchen, hand braced against the door frame.

"Sure. Chinese sounds good."

"I have to move some boxes into the attic, but when I get back I'll order."

Timothy nodded. "Tell me how much and I'll pitch in."

For a moment, Wyatt wanted to say, *You don't have to, she's not your mother.* But that would come out far harsher than he meant it. "Sure. I'll let you know." He ducked back into the hall.

His mother's apartment was on the second floor. It took him a few minutes to find the door that led to the attic. Once he did, it wasn't as bad as he thought it might be. The stairs and attic space were well-lit at least, not just by the ceiling lights but also from a circular window set into the front of the house that let the last of the day's sunlight and warmth spill in. It was dusty up there, but not dirty per se, and the floor felt sturdy under him, which made it about a hundred percent safer than the attic of the old farmhouse where he'd grown up.

Wyatt shifted the boxes one at a time up the stairs. It was hard to tell where to put them because everything in the attic seemed to be randomly arranged, without any clear way of identifying what belonged to whom. He opted to push his mother's boxes back as far as they would go against the wall opposite the stairs—although he ended up having to stack them near the window simply because that was the only space left.

The closer he got to the window, the hotter it got, causing pricking points of sweat to break out along

5

his arms and the back of his neck. His eyes began to water against the light and dust, and when he'd moved the last box up Wyatt sat cross-legged on the floor.

He should go back down and order Chinese or see how book sorting was going. Instead, he tipped his face back and closed his eyes, taking several deep breaths.

They'd been at the old house packing until one or two o'clock in the morning. Then Timothy had arrived with the truck at five. Wyatt's limbs were heavy, the muscles in his back ached with every move, and they still had the entire apartment to unpack. He rotated his shoulders, trying to get the kinks out.

From the stairs, Jess's laugh, loud and strong, drifted up, his mother's laughter, too, thank God.

It was ... strange, though, hearing them down there with him alone up here.

He stood up, trying to brush dust off his ass as he did, and didn't realize he'd misjudged until pain exploded bright and hot behind his eyes. Wood, dust, and dirt showered down on top of him. "Shit!" He doubled over, hands going to the back of his head, which he'd rammed straight into a beam. "Fuck!"

The first shock gave way to waves of pain encompassing his entire head, bad enough to make his eyes fill with tears. He went back down onto his knees and for a moment thought maybe he should start screaming for Jess, who was a nurse after all. The pain was already lessening, though, so Wyatt just rocked back and forth while groaning pitifully.

Eventually, it diminished to the point that he could take his hands away, inspect them carefully for blood, and stand back up.

Some of the pink insulation had gotten loose right above where his head hit the beam, but otherwise nothing looked any worse for the wear. You weren't supposed to touch insulation, if he remembered correctly, but on the other hand he didn't want to leave pieces hanging out. He pulled the sleeve of his flannel shirt over his hand and tried to stuff the insulation back into the ceiling. Of course it didn't go back in easily. Wyatt put his full weight behind it and shoved up arm first as hard as he could. The entire thing crunched, and then a large piece fell out, landing at his feet.

"Well, fuck." Wyatt looked accusingly at the hole he'd made.

There was something behind the insulation. He reached up, fingertips brushing paper. He pushed his hand farther in until he could feel an edge and then pulled. The whole thing came away at once.

It was an envelope, one of the large ones people used to send papers in, brittle and already falling to pieces as he held it. It felt too light to contain papers. Wyatt opened it as carefully as he could.

There didn't seem to be anything in there when he inched his fingers in, so he turned it upside down to be sure. He squeezed the bottom and shook the envelope several times. Something fell out and fluttered to the floor.

Wyatt bent to pick it up.

It was a photograph. Not a particularly large one, a little bit faded, the corners slightly tattered.

Two men sat, one darker skinned and one fairer, each on opposite sides of a table but facing the camera rather than each other. They wore matching dark suits and posed almost identically, with one hand resting on the tabletop. The light-skinned man's legs were crossed, his pose more relaxed. His companion stared straight at the camera. He seemed almost nervous in his tense focus, in the way he held himself. Neither of them smiled, but there was something almost candid about the shot, as if the men were waiting for the actual portrait to be taken. As if the moment after this one, the fairer man had uncrossed his legs, sat up straighter, while his companion had loosened his pose, letting some of that energy go, sitting with more confidence. In this moment, though, the two were caught in anticipation.

The back of Wyatt's neck pricked, and he turned the photograph over, but there was nothing to see there. He picked the envelope up again and inspected it. It was truly empty this time and also completely unmarked.

What kind of photograph got stuck in an envelope and shoved up into the ceiling of someone's attic?

He looked at it again, the two of them sitting there, caught in that moment, both of them unguarded, their hands slid a little too close together on the table.

Maybe the better question was, *What kind of photograph do you hide?*

Wyatt stared for another second and then shook his head. It was probably nothing, just an old picture that had been forgotten about.

There was something about the two of them, though. His finger went to trace the shape of the fairer one, the angle of his jaw, the way the light outlined his face—it felt *family* in a way that resonated deep inside Wyatt's body.

"Who were you?" He kept his voice low. "Were you hiding?"

There were, of course, the obvious theories, reasons a picture like this might be put away. He could imagine that they had been a couple. This one incriminating piece of evidence tucked away to keep it from being destroyed after the deaths of the people it portrayed.

Wyatt had never hidden being queer, but when it came to everything else, all he did was hide.

9

The weight of passing through the world as some-thing he was not was almost crushing sometimes. For people to look at him and see a man when he so clearly wasn't felt like the worst kind of lie. It was like having an empty place inside of you, a rough, torn-out spot to be guarded, hidden, lied about. A bruise you could forget even hurt until it was touched.

Had *they* known?

He tucked the photograph into his breast pocket and descended the stairs to his mother's new apartment.

The town hall of Windsor, New York, was a particu-larly unimpressive building: low, and quite small.

Then again, the township itself was tiny, mostly farmland. Main Street consisted of a church, a bank, and a really sketchy bar.

Wyatt parked his car in the tiny parking lot next to the building and leaned over to pick a brochure off the passenger seat. "Brochure" was being generous to the piece of paper he'd printed off the Internet.

It said "Windsor Historical Society" across the front, with a black-and-white, and now slightly smudgy, sketch of the building in front of him. Wind-sor was about twenty minutes from his home in Binghamton. He'd picked it because it was the only historical society in the area whose business hours didn't conflict with his work schedule.

According to the brochure, the actual historical society was in the basement, but you could access it from a side door.

Wyatt stuffed the printout into his satchel and got out of the car. He picked his way across the gravel parking lot in the light of early morning, just hoping he hadn't made the trip for no reason.

Side door, he learned after a quick walk around the building, meant *concrete staircase leading down to an old metal storm door propped open with a rock.*

Wyatt pulled the door farther open and peered down a long, narrow, dimly lit hallway with another door at the far end. He dug out the brochure again and double-checked it. He did appear to be the right place, as dubious as it looked. He told himself it wasn't that bad, but his pace quickened.

Windsor Historical Society was stenciled on the door at the end of the hall. The door itself looked battered and old, but when Wyatt tried the handle it opened.

He stepped through into a surprisingly large, high-ceilinged room with a tiled floor, completely filled with things. A bookcase overflowed with books, old display cases showed off everything from yellowed clothes hanging on dusty dummies to silverware, teacups, and journals. Several long tables were set up in the center of the room, each piled high with books and shoeboxes, notecards and three-ring binders. Filing cabinets and card catalogs sectioned off one corner of the room, over which Wyatt could see a desk with a huge nineties-style computer that looked to be the newest thing in the room. It was as though a library and a museum had suffered a head-on collision.

"Can I help you?"

A man stood by another doorway at the far end of the room. Wyatt made the first logical guess. "Grayson Alexander?"

"Yes?"

Wyatt found himself hunching. At over six feet, he towered over everyone, but he tried not to be an asshole about it. "Wyatt Kelly. I have a photograph." He stuck out his hand for Grayson to take.

Grayson was shorter than him, a compact, barrel-chested guy. His dark red hair curled into his face, softening his features. He wore a bowtie and waistcoat, clothes Wyatt generally didn't see outside of steampunk cosplay. Yet Grayson seemed unironic, or maybe unapologetic, about it. Fearlessness in self-expression was rare, in Wyatt's experience. He felt a warmth start inside him, both attraction and recognition of a sort.

Grayson's hand was soft in Wyatt's, his handshake firm.

"Do you have the photograph with you?" Grayson crossed his arms when Wyatt let go.

"Oh." Wyatt had been so caught up in looking, he hadn't taken the photograph out. He dug in his satchel again and came up with it in a plastic sandwich bag. "Here." He handed it over. Grayson held it by the edges as he examined it.

"I found it in the attic of the house my mom just moved into." Wyatt watched Grayson. Did he see what Wyatt had seen? The emotion and expectant stillness caught up within the image? "It's a big old Victorian that's been broken up for apartments. The landlord said we could use the attic for storage. I found it up there."

"You don't know who these men are?" Grayson turned the picture over and leaned in close, studying the back.

"No, I couldn't figure out who they were. That's why I thought of taking it to a historical society." Wyatt hadn't even known where to start, actually. He'd mentioned it to the landlord when he told him about the hole he'd made. The landlord had been completely uninterested in the photograph or what Wyatt did with it. "I thought it was interesting when I found it. It was stuck up in the ceiling behind the insulation. It seemed strange to find a photograph there, like it was hidden or something. I don't know, it made me want to know more about who they were and why they were up there in the first place." His face heated as he spoke. He was rambling.

Grayson looked up. His eyes were very green, and Wyatt couldn't help but notice the smattering of freckles across his nose.

He gripped the photograph delicately. "Well, it's in good condition, not a whole lot of fading, no scratching or tearing." He turned it over again, examining the edges closely. "It doesn't look like it's been trimmed or mounted in a scrapbook." He carried the photograph to his desk and held it under the lamp there.

Wyatt followed and half leaned over his shoulder, trying not to crowd too close. Grayson stared down at the two figures, and for a moment Wyatt thought that Grayson *knew*. It made his pulse speed up and his body tense, just a little bit.

"From their clothes, I would say it's from around the nineteen-tens, maybe a little bit earlier. The photograph itself is on a little bit of stiffer stock like real photograph postcard, which would have been a cheaper, easier way to get a portrait done. The only thing is it doesn't have a postcard back." Grayson flipped it over, and they both bent to peer at the blank side of the photograph. "It could have still been done by a photographer who would have ordinarily done postcards though, so that's a place to start." He straightened and looked at Wyatt again. "You need to know, though, that it's going to be difficult to find out who these two are. It can be tricky identifying people from photographs when we don't know who took the picture, when it was taken, or where."

"Okay." Wyatt tried to keep smiling, even as his heart sank with disappointment.

He didn't know what he'd expected, but he'd hoped the two man would be identifiable—and then, once he'd gotten here, he'd hoped that Grayson would understand.

Grayson looked a little apologetic. "I'm sorry, I just don't want you to get your hopes up about something I might not be able to do."

"It's all right." As unhappy as Wyatt would be if Grayson didn't unearth anything, he couldn't demand Grayson produce what wasn't there to find. "Whatever you can dig up will be good enough for me."

"I will try." The way he looked up at Wyatt was earnest. "It's a lovely photograph. What's the address of the house where you found it?"

Wyatt tried to gather his thoughts, shoving away the jumble of emotions to deal with later. "Sixty-two James Street in Binghamton."

Grayson jotted it down. "May I take a picture of this?" He held up the photograph.

Wyatt blinked. "Sure."

Grayson put the picture down on his desk and pulled out his cell phone. He snapped several pictures before handing the sandwich bag back to Wyatt.

"All right." Grayson turned to rummage through the piles of papers and books on either side of the computer. He pulled out a slightly wrinkled business card that included something the historical society website had not listed: an email address.

Wyatt dug into his satchel and pulled out a business card of his own. "Here."

Grayson took the card. "I'll email you if I find anything. And you should feel free to email me if you have any other questions."

"I'll remember that." Wyatt slipped the card into his pocket.

Grayson just nodded, turning back toward his computer. So Wyatt let himself out of the over-crowded basement room and headed for his car.

Work kept him later than he would have liked, and his phone began to buzz almost as soon as he stepped out of the county government office building and onto the street. When he saw his sister's name, he answered. "Hey, what's up?"

"Can you check on Mom?"

Wyatt tensed. "Is there something wrong?"

"No, I just think she's lonely in that apartment by herself. I have a late shift tonight, so I was wondering if you could swing by instead."

"Of course." Wyatt dug out his car keys one-handed.

"And while you're there, make sure she's taking her meds."

He heard cars in the background, and sirens. Jess was probably at the hospital where she worked.

"Just don't …" She sighed. He could imagine her rubbing her fingers across her forehead. "Don't force it or make her feel bad. Just take a quick look at her organizer. I filled it up on Sunday. Make sure the right compartments are empty."

"Yeah." Wyatt quickened his pace into the parking garage.

There was the sound of someone talking on her end, too faint for Wyatt to really hear. "I've got to get back to work." She sounded distracted now, a little harried. "Thanks for this."

Wyatt stopped, hand on his car door. "It's not a problem. You know I'm always going to be there for her, and you, too."

"Aw." Her voice went teasing. "Give me a call later tonight, would you? About the pills."

"Yep." He slid into the driver's seat. "Love you."

"Love you, too." Wyatt could hear her smile.

The sun was setting by the time he pulled up to his mom's apartment, the sky a light gray flecked through with blue.

His mom answered on his first knock. "Hey." He hugged her. "You look good today."

She did, too, dressed in a long skirt and peasant blouse reminiscent of his childhood, with large earrings and beads.

"Hello, yourself." She waved him into the apartment. "I didn't know you were coming over."

"I thought I'd stop by." Wyatt balanced on one foot in the hall, wrestling off his dress shoes and hanging up his coat. "And also Jess called."

Her eyebrows furrowed, and Wyatt froze, cold seeping through him. *Please let her remember Jess.*

"What did Jess say?"

Just like that, he could breathe again. "She wanted me to check in with you."

She tsked, turning back toward the kitchen. "She worries too much."

Wyatt smiled at that. "I know, but I thought we could have dinner. It could be fun, right?"

"Of course. I was just going to heat something up, but if you're staying, we could make something. It's been a long time since we cooked together." She gave him a smile that pulled at the center of him. It said *home, safe, loved.* On impulse, he leaned down and hugged her. "Hey." She hugged him back.

"That sounds great. Let's cook." He tugged her into the kitchen and started rolling up his sleeves. "What have you got that we can use?"

"I don't know." Frowning, she started poking through the fridge, freezer, and cupboards.

Wyatt told himself it was okay, that he didn't remember what exactly was in his fridge half the time either. Plus, Jess had been the one to take Mom shopping last time, so Wyatt didn't have any idea what she should have around the kitchen.

She rummaged through the cupboards over the counter by the stove. Wyatt opened the refrigerator. There was a green pepper and a carton of mushrooms in the drawer, along with a package of ground beef on the top shelf. He piled the ingredients on the counter while his mother pulled a jar of pasta sauce and a box of spaghetti from the cupboard.

The obvious answer to dinner was spaghetti and meatballs. Wyatt knelt down to pull out pots and pans while his mother began to chop the vegetables. They moved around each other in the echo of an older rhythm. At one point, they'd cooked together almost every night, but not for a long time, and never in this kitchen. It was different from the house he'd grown up in. The stove didn't pop and groan when you tried to light it, and the kitchen island his mother had made out of found wood hadn't come with them. This kitchen was clean, new, and compact—the stove electric, the counters barely touched. Only the table was the same, old and heavy, the wood marked all over by time.

Her hands were as sure as they'd ever been as she sliced the onion. Wyatt stood next to her dutifully at

19

the stove. He could imagine they were back home. She'd give him a glass of wine and ask about college or work as she moved around, cooking and tidying. Jess would be late, because she was always late. Wyatt would stir the pots on the stove while his mother chopped vegetables and checked the food in the oven.

To spend their time together wishing things were like they had been wasn't fair to either of them, though. Wyatt shifted away from the stove to let her scrape the onions into one of the pans.

She put the chopping board back on the counter and looked over at him. "So how is work?"

"It's fine." Wyatt hated to be cryptic with his family about the job, but he worked for a judge. "Long and boring today. I did mostly research, then went to a hearing and took notes."

She hummed a little to herself. "But they keep you busy, and that's good."

"Yeah, they do."

She was quiet again, stirring the ingredients together and forming them into balls. The sauce simmered on the stove with the added pepper and mushrooms.

The kitchen windows clouded with steam from the spaghetti pot. The smell of onions, browning meat, and the tang of tomato sauce filled the room as his mother transferred the meatballs into a pan.

Wyatt unfolded a tablecloth, green with white flowers, and smoothed it over the kitchen table. He pulled her white china from the cupboard as she started taking things off the stove.

"Do you need help with that?" He watched her lift the heavy skillet filled with bubbling sauce and meatballs.

"I've got it." She poured its contents into a serving bowl. "If you could finish setting the table, that would be lovely."

He made sure she had the skillet back on the stove before he finished putting down the silverware. They carried food to the table together before seating themselves one at each end.

"So how is it going with ..." She paused for a moment as if in thought, scooping spaghetti onto her plate as she did. "I'm sorry, honey, I don't remember his name, the boy you're dating."

"We broke up a couple months ago. I told you." Wyatt let her serve him spaghetti as well, before ladling sauce over it.

"Oh, well." She reached over and patted his arm. "You'll find someone new, or ..." She narrowed her eyes at him, speculating. "You're not dating anyone you haven't told me about, right?"

For a moment he was sixteen again, rolling his eyes and turning bright red with embarrassment. "No, Mom."

She raised a hand. "Not that you have to tell me everything. You're grown now. But I would hope that if you were dating someone, you'd bring him around sometime to see me."

"Of course I would."

Would he? Before, he always had, but now? *She's sick*, he reminded himself, angry he'd even questioned it. *Not dead, not an embarrassment*. God, what was wrong with him?

"You're a good man." Her gaze was brimming with kindness and understanding, and that hurt worst of all. "And I'm not just saying that because I'm your mother. You'll meet a nice man, like Jess."

Wyatt looked down at his plate, his appetite gone. He could acknowledge how lucky he was to have the support of his family when it came to his sexuality. She hadn't even blinked when he'd come out at fifteen. It had been such a nonissue, so anticlimactic, he'd walked around for weeks waiting for the other shoe to drop.

Would you be just as supportive if I told you I wasn't a boy? He swallowed, his throat gone dry. *Would you be all right not having a son—having just a child instead?* His stomach churned around the food he'd just put in it.

He tried not to think about that, to concentrate on the here and now. "You want to watch a movie? Or TV? Isn't that singing show you like on tonight?"

"Is it?" She lit up. "I hadn't realized, I thought it wasn't on for a few more days."

Wyatt pulled out his phone. "Let me check." He leaned on the table while he pulled up the show's schedule. "No, it's on tonight. Should we watch it?"

"If you don't mind."

Wyatt smiled. "Yeah, let's, I've not been keeping track, so you'll have to tell me who to root for."

She smiled back. "Deal."

They took the dishes to the sink, and Wyatt loaded the dishwasher. "You want to go get set up?" He nodded to the living room.

"You sure you don't need any more help?"

"I'm good. Can you work the TV? Or should I do it?"

"I can do it."

Wyatt waited until she'd left before reaching for the medication organizer. It seemed to be okay. All the right medication was missing. He would have to assume she'd taken it. Besides, she seemed lucid, which supported the theory that she was on her medication like she was supposed to be.

God, how much longer could she live by herself? What would they do when she couldn't get through a day without help? He put the medication back and set the last of the dishes in the dishwasher, tidied up the leftovers, and wiped down the table. There had been a time when she'd never have left the kitchen with the table still dirty, no matter how many times he offered to do it.

But today had been good, today had been fine. He needed to hold on to every good day, every good moment, with no way of knowing how many more there would be. They said Alzheimer's was so much more treatable now than it had been, but that was still so far from all right.

A little water from the dishcloth he'd used to clean the table had gotten on his hands. He wiped them on his slacks.

It would be fine, though, it would be fine, it was all going to be fine.

Wyatt realized he'd been wiping his hands over and over on the legs of his slacks. He let them drop to his sides.

"Wyatt," his mother called from the living room, "do you remember what channel it's going to be on?"

"I'm pretty sure we're watching it on Hulu." He turned toward the doorway. "Wait a minute, and I'll set it up."

The icy rain that had been pelting the area for the last two weeks had given way to snow when Grayson pulled himself out of bed. He stumbled down the hall from his bedroom into the kitchen.

The snow lay wetly across the stubble and bare ground of the cornfield across the street. He could hear the wet flakes hitting the ice already covering the roof of his trailer home.

The snow also covered his car in a deep, heavy slush. It was going to be a joy scraping that off and convincing his elderly engine to turn over.

There was one tree in front of his house that usually shaded his car, but it was weighed down with thick gray snow and covered in crows. A visual representation of how deeply unpleasant going out in this weather would be.

It was Thursday, though, which meant he had work at the historical society—the one day out of the week that he could be himself—so the roads would have to be impassable for him to miss it.

He leaned against the counter in the kitchen and watched the old drip coffeemaker halfheartedly spit coffee into the pot. He kept meaning to buy a new one, but then he'd end up spending a little extra money on food or gas, or it would be one of the kids' birthdays or the electric bill would be high, and he'd think, *Next week*. If he just waited and saved, he'd have money for a more expensive one that would make better coffee and last longer. But truthfully, next week was never going to be better, and saving was a lost cause. He needed to buckle down and pick up another cheap plastic one.

With the coffeemaker doing its thing, he went to shower and dress.

In the bedroom, his binder lay still tangled with his clothes from the day before. Grayson pulled it free of his shirt and put it on the bed. Technically, if the binder left marks, you weren't supposed to wear it again. Maybe dudes who were ramrod thin and had A-cup breasts could wear a semifunctional binder without striping up their torso, but every binder he'd ever owned cut into the top of his belly and left red stripes across his love handles. Not to mention it didn't even get him flat. There was just no way to disguise Ds, he thought as he wrestled the binder over the fat rolls on his back. He pulled on an undershirt once he'd successfully fought the binder into submission, and a dress shirt over all of what he was already wearing. He would give an arm to be able to afford top surgery, but it was yet another thing he was failing to save up for.

Suspenders today, he decided once in his bedroom, and a bowtie, along with his favorite gray herringbone blazer. One of the good things about working by himself in the basement was he could wear whatever he wanted without worrying that people would talk.

He pulled on his boots and coat, picked up his bag, and stamped out to the car to brush the snow off it. In the tree, the flock of crows clacked at each other and screamed in shrill, jagged pieces of sound. Grayson swore at them as he dumped an armful of wet snow onto the ground.

His car choked to life after a few minutes of cajoling, and he slowly backed out of his driveway, praying the roads had been plowed and salted already. They had not, but he managed to make it to the Windsor town hall without sliding off the road anyway.

He unlocked the door and hung up the welcome sign.

After sitting down, he brought up the photograph on his computer. He hadn't used photographs much in school. There had been a couple of media studies classes where he'd used movies, but not a whole lot of photographs.

But then again, Wyatt had just asked to know who the two men were, not for an in-depth analysis.

Grayson fired up the Internet. The Binghamton Historical Society was a lot bigger than his, with more staff and resources. They'd be in better shape to track down whoever was in the picture.

Before he could email them, though, he needed to get a rough idea of when it had been taken.

He Googled "nineteenth-century male couple," which got him almost nothing useful. "Victorian male couple" ended up being much more useful— though Grayson was pretty sure most of the photographs were British, which did him no good. Still, he tried to compare clothing and the backdrop to the photograph he had to the ones on the computer.

It didn't help that a lot of the photographs on the Internet were vaguely labeled things like "two men posed together late 19th century." As if Grayson couldn't clearly see that by just looking at the picture.

Wyatt's photograph was also printed on paper that hadn't yellowed as badly as most of the pre-1880s photographs Grayson had seen. It looked more like the ones from the early 1900s to 1930s, as he'd guessed. So Grayson made a note: "Presumed to be 1900s–1920."

If the photograph was taken during the early twentieth century, then the Binghamton Historical Society would probably have a good idea of who at least the black man in the picture was.

Both men looked to be middle class or lower middle class, judging from their suits. That meant that if the men were local, there was a very good chance they had worked for George F. Johnson. In the early part of the twentieth century, there just couldn't have been that many black employees of Endicott Johnson Corporation.

He sent off a scanned copy of the picture, his estimated dates, and where the picture had been found with a short message to the Binghamton staff.

That done, he looked again at his copy of the photograph.

These same-sex portraits were interesting. They were so common, but there was startlingly little research on them.

When he'd been in school, Grayson had specialized in queer history. He'd used a lot more court records, military records, newspaper articles, and other more traditional sources than he had photographs, though.

Usually scholarship taught that these photographs could depict one man sitting on the other's lap without it being gay—or so the theory went. That these kinds of pictures needed to be interpreted as evidence of homosocial friendship and not romantic or sexual intimacy. The burden then fell on the scholar to *prove* the subjects' queerness.

Carroll Smith Rosenberg's "Female World of Love and Ritual" had been the article to pioneer that argument, as far as Grayson knew. He should track down a copy and refresh his memory. Setting the photograph aside, he pulled up the spreadsheet he used to catalog genealogy information he'd gotten requests for.

When he heard back from the Binghamton Historical Society, he could do more work on the photo.

CHAPTER 2

Grayson kicked off his boots as soon as he got home and put his satchel next to the desk before going to turn on lights and start water for tea.

Living in such a small space meant it heated up quickly and stayed warm in the winter. His little furnace chugged, and Grayson's water boiled. He fixed himself tea, then carried the mug, laptop, and his work bag over to the couch and settled himself down.

The Binghamton Historical Society had come through for him. They'd been able to pull up a name for the black man in the picture: James Miller.

Grayson took a sip of tea and read the email more closely. Unsurprisingly, James had worked for George F. Johnson, who'd singlehandedly employed most of the population of Binghamton at one time. Johnson City was named after him. Grayson had grown up in the Binghamton area and just took it for granted that everything had Johnson's name on it. Parks were named after him, and the church had been built using his money, as had many of the libraries and schools. Binghamton and its surrounding townships had been solid factory towns in the nineteenth century. In a factory town, everything belonged to the factory boss, and Johnson was the biggest factory boss of them all.

James Miller had been listed as an accountant for George F. Johnson, or more particularly his company. He had been slightly above a bookkeeper, but not by much. The Binghamton Historical Society had no records on where James was born, where he'd died, if he'd married, or what kind of education he had—though he must have had some education, judging by his job.

That was it. Almost nothing. There was so little, Grayson rather suspected that James had at some point moved away from the Binghamton area. Which was the problem with doing local history—it pretty much only worked as long as the people you were researching stayed local. If James had moved, he would have totally disappeared from the records Grayson had access to. Without knowing where exactly James had gone, finding him would be almost impossible. Or he could have died young or become estranged from his family at some point, which could also explain the silence. Generally, white middle-class people wove in and out of the historical record; everyone else skimmed below recorded history.

That was why Grayson had always preferred doing research on ideas and social concepts. They were easy to follow, leaving marks on everything from advertisements to media to literature.

Power in general cut deep swaths through history, marking, scarring, and claiming everything it touched. It disfigured people, turning them into characters who had never really existed at all. It crushed places into dust and built castles of dreams, lies, and fantasies. It warped events until trying to see through the lies was like trying to see using only a broken mirror. And the worst part was, power, in its own ways, always told the truth. The history of power in both its glory and its corruption was an easy kind of history to do.

Looking beneath it into the quagmire of lives, possibilities, and stories was so much harder. So often, there was nothing left to find. In this case, maybe just a photograph of two mildly attractive but ultimately nameless people.

Though one now had a name.

Grayson set his computer aside. He wandered into the kitchen and started to take things out of the refrigerator for the curry he was going to make for dinner.

He wondered if he could locate James by going through army records. Was there some kind of connection to do with military service between him and the other man? The other man could be a relative. James wasn't known to have had any brothers, but the man could be a cousin. Or they could have been business partners. The photograph didn't even need to be local in origin. It could have been taken anywhere and then sent back to Binghamton.

There were just too many questions and variables.

He was going to have to explain that to Wyatt, he thought, as he chopped an onion and spinach. Sometimes when you did historical research, you hit a dead end and that was that—nothing more to find. Still, it was going to hurt to tell Wyatt. He'd been so excited to identify the people in this photograph.

Well, Grayson had found one of them. That at least would be something to give Wyatt.

He transferred onions, garlic, and spinach from the cutting board into the pan on the stove. The mixture hissed and steamed as he reached for a spatula.

How many people would have thrown that photograph away when they'd found it? Tucked it somewhere and forgotten about it, or even sold it on the Internet? There were thousands upon thousands of these kinds of pictures floating around, cheaply made, depicting people who had long since been forgotten. Grayson could go to any antique store and find a photograph of this age and quality for only a few dollars. This one wasn't a family heirloom, and it certainly wasn't worth any money. Yet it was important to Wyatt, and interesting enough for him to take it all the way to Grayson's little historical society.

It made a knot form in Grayson's stomach to think about the conversation they were going to have. He added spices to the pan and stirred it again. He had to be realistic with both of them about this project and this sort of research. At the same time, it felt like he was letting Wyatt down.

He needed to just get it over with—the sooner the better. After dinner, he'd email Wyatt.

The sun was low in the sky, burning orange and gold across the water of the river when Wyatt finally pulled into his own driveway. Once inside, he stripped off his work clothes and put on jeans and an oversized sweater before getting himself a glass of wine and settling on the couch.

There was an email from Grayson when he opened his computer.

Dear Mr. Kelly,

I have a small amount of information about the picture you gave me. I would suggest we meet at

Starbucks to talk about it. Please let me know when you will be free to meet.

Sincerely,

Grayson Alexander

Wyatt got that fluttery feeling in his chest. Grayson wanted to meet. For coffee, not just to email back and forth.

It's not a date, Wyatt told himself. He needed to keep that in mind. Also, did he want to date Grayson anyway? Was it because Grayson was trans? Because Wyatt was pretty sure Grayson was trans. The shape of the body didn't tell everyone everything — Wyatt knew that all too well. But there was something about Grayson, the way Wyatt had felt when he'd seen him. He'd just known.

When it came to trans people, he usually knew, no matter how stealth, real or passing. Like he'd been reaching out for something for so long, he didn't realize he still had his hand extended until someone reached back.

But connecting was not the same as romantic attraction. And having the feeling that someone was trans wasn't the same as knowing.

Unease settled on him when he thought about the way some binary trans people were toward non-binary trans people like him. Would Grayson see *him*?

Geeky, awkward, unsure, but also with a nice smile, pretty hands—and Wyatt liked to think he was funny and could make a mean lasagna.

Or would Grayson just see a man in a dress?

Anxiety twisted around his heart like a bramble, making him feel nauseated.

He needed to think about something else, like the photograph. What had Grayson found? Did he know who the men were?

Wyatt hoped he'd found them and that the story behind the picture was as interesting as he imagined it was.

He dug the photograph out, still in its sandwich bag, and looked at it. There was the way they sat, the placement of their hands, but Wyatt got caught all over again by the eyes. The darker one's eyes were so intense, his gaze steady yet a little unsure. His companion held himself with more self-assurance, although there was a vulnerability, too. He looked like someone made helpless by things not said, and it made Wyatt's heart hurt, his whole body longing for things he couldn't have.

It felt good to see part of himself like this. Even this part, or maybe particularly this part, laid here in the gaze of a stranger who had surely been dead for decades. Time made it feel at once both distant and intimate.

It was possible, here in his living room, for Wyatt to look at this photograph and think about the things that usually were too big and too much to handle.

"Were you like me?" He asked the one with the closed-off gaze especially. "Did you know this? Would you have understood?" He took a sip of wine and then set the glass next to the photograph on the coffee table.

"Every time I go to tell my mom," he told them both, "I always talk myself out of it. I tell myself it's for the best, that she doesn't need to know, no one does, but deep down, I think it's because I'm scared of losing her. Which ... is so stupid. I'm going to lose her anyway." It wasn't something he admitted often, and almost never out loud, but keeping the words inside of you didn't make them any less real.

He curled in on himself, arms around legs pulled up tight against his chest.

CHAPTER 3

For a city with multiple colleges, there was a definite dearth of coffee shops in the Binghamton area.

Grayson had chosen the one and only Starbucks in town, across the street from the community college.

Even though Broome Community College was pretty working-class, the Starbucks was filled with hipster boys and white girls at the point in their lives when they thought dreads were a good idea. Generally, Grayson thought he blended in fairly well in university and college spaces. He should have stood out less here than pretty much anywhere else in Binghamton except maybe on the university campus.

Yet he was being stared at.

Even though Grayson wasn't looking, he could feel their eyes on him. He turned his head just enough to see the table across the room with its little collection of people, all watching him.

They didn't look local, definitely not affiliated with the college. They were all in their thirties, the women tastefully made up, with hair that looked expensive and nice manicures. The guys wore very plain but equally very expensive suits and large, ostentatious watches. Maybe they were on their way back from a trip Upstate to their homes in New York City, Long Island, Westchester County—wherever they made people like that. Certainly not here. He turned his head very deliberately to look straight at them and glared.

Most of the people at the table looked away immediately, the ladies ducking their heads like they knew they'd done something wrong. One man kept right on staring at him. The dude was dark-haired, tall, broad-shouldered and barrel-chested in his fancy suit.

Grayson didn't look away, but he stiffened, his back straightening even as he fought the urge to hunch. The desire to both fight and flee was strong.

A hand landed on his shoulder, and he jumped.

It was Wyatt. He looked a little taken aback. "I'm sorry for startling you. Am I interrupting something?"

"No. Sit." He curled his fingers around the warm cardboard of his disposable coffee cup and tried to relax as Wyatt folded himself into the chair across from him.

Wyatt wore skinny jeans today, boots, an untucked blue oxford shirt, a gray houndstooth sweater. Chunky glasses framed his very dark eyes. He looked good, actually.

"So"—Grayson tested the words he wanted to say in his mind before he let them fall out of his mouth—"I've done some research into the photograph. And I have to say, I've hit a dead end."

Wyatt frowned. "What do you mean, 'dead end'?"

"Sometimes when you do historical research you find all the answers you were looking for and a boat-load of other questions besides, and sometimes you don't." He unwrapped his hands from the coffee cup and spread them flat on the surface of the table. "The black man in the photograph I believe to be James Miller." Grayson pointed to him. "He worked as a bookkeeper for George F. Johnson, and that's about all I know. And in my professional opinion I've found all there is to find. I'm sorry."

"There has to be more. People don't …" He made a vague gesture in the air between them. "… disappear."

"Of course they do." Grayson folded his hands on the table. "They disappear all the time right now, let alone when there's at least a hundred years between us and them. Things disappear: papers, letters, journals, photographs. Things get lost, thrown out, destroyed. Most of what we work with in history survived through sheer luck, and James Miller is just gone." He sighed. The best thing was to get it out on the table. "I can do a little more looking, but the reality is that finding more than what we've already got is extremely unlikely. This is just all there is."

Wyatt opened his mouth as if he was about to say something and then closed it. When their gazes met, he looked lost.

Then he straightened back up and plastered on a smile Grayson didn't believe. "All right. Well, thank you."

Grayson wanted to reach out, to comfort him in some way, but he wasn't sure it would be welcome. He kept his hands folded. "It wasn't a problem. I enjoyed doing it." Grayson found he meant it, too. "And if I do find anything else, anything at all, I'll contact you right away. If you find anything, let me know." He smiled up at Wyatt, and Wyatt smiled back. It was a small victory.

"Of course." Wyatt ducked his head, still smiling a little, and then reached into his pocket when his phone vibrated. He touched the screen, then frowned at it. "I'm sorry, but I have work." He looked tired now, and his tone was genuinely apologetic.

"Don't let me keep you." Grayson gave him a small, dismissive wave and a smile, this one more forced than the last.

Wyatt stood, taking his coffee with him. "See you."

"See you around." Wyatt gave him another small smile before turning toward the exit.

The glass door closed behind him. The people across the room were watching again, this time pretending like they weren't.

Grayson dumped his now-cool coffee in the garbage can on his way out.

It was snowing, big wet flakes falling from a light gray sky. The road was thick with a mix of wet snow.

Wyatt lived over in Port Dickinson Township, which had once been an upscale neighborhood. Like everything in Binghamton, it now showed signs of rust and decay, although it was still quiet and safe. Most of the houses had once been solid, middle-class family homes with manicured lawns. A good number had been broken up into apartments, and the area was starting to look ragged around the edges.

Wyatt rented half of a beautiful red brick house with a slate roof. It had one bedroom, and the floors were hardwood. The bathroom was huge, with a claw-foot tub. The tub had clinched the deal as far as Wyatt was concerned. The house was gorgeous, the apartment twice as large as any he'd lived in before.

The other half was rented by a lovely dude about his own age toiling away at his dissertation, the dude's equally lovely wife, and their year-old daughter.

Really, though, it had been all about the tub.

Their backyard looked straight down onto the river, but they were up high enough that they'd been spared the worst of the 2006 and 2011 floods.

He kicked his boots off and shucked his jacket before heading for the bedroom to get out of his work clothes.

He'd been retiling the kitchen floor with his landlord's blessing, doing it over in soft heather green, but right now he had only half a tiled floor, with a whole lot of stacks of tiles just lying in wait for him to trip over. He collected a bottle of wine and a glass and went back into the living room.

On the coffee table next to his laptop and a stack of coasters was the photograph of James Miller. Wyatt sat on the couch and poured himself a glass of wine while he stared at it.

Grayson had said there wasn't anything more to find, but Wyatt couldn't believe that was true. How could there be nothing more to find?

He slid the photograph closer, feeling how stiff and brittle the paper was under his fingers.

Maybe he should do some research of his own. He reached for his computer, pulled up Google, and paused. What did historians do?

He had no idea. Grayson had talked a lot about research, but Wyatt didn't even know where to start. The last time he'd studied history had been in college, Introduction to American History I and II. It had been a lot like social studies class in high school, and they'd basically just read from a textbook.

They'd done research in law classes, of course, but laws were easy to find in archives on websites or in reference books in the library.

Well, the library was probably the best place to start, so Wyatt Googled the Broome County library system. Typing in "James Miller" gave him nothing, as did typing in "Miller family." Wyatt sighed and reached for his wine. He should have known. If it had been that easy, Grayson would have already done it. Grayson was a professional, after all, with years more experience and education than Wyatt had.

If he couldn't do it, what do you think you're doing?

Wyatt ignored that thought and clicked on the link at the top of the page marked "local history." He flipped through newspaper archives and census records, but he had no idea where to even start.

He went back to the catalog search and typed in "Binghamton." A long list of books came up. Wyatt was excited for a moment before realizing that most of the books either weren't owned by the library or weren't about Binghamton, New York. There were a few histories, though, and quite a few collections of pictures of Binghamton and other places in Broome County. He noted down the titles and call numbers, then Googled "Binghamton history."

Most of the sites that popped up were not particularly useful, but he did find *Binghamton: A Brief History*, which seemed like a good place to start.

It gave him some interesting facts, like that Binghamton was named after William Bingham, a businessman from Philadelphia who had bought the area in 1786 for agricultural and industrial purposes. As far as Wyatt could tell, the Onondaga's and Oneida's original towns had been destroyed by American soldiers, and the area had been used for producing goods and materials to be taken somewhere else, usually New York City. There were also lots of pictures of women in Victorian-style dresses staring dubiously at the camera as they made shoes for George F. Johnson's shoe empire.

Binghamton was at one point called "the Parlor City" because of the community of businessmen who made it big in industry and owned fancy houses in the area. The website had pictures of these houses, some of which Wyatt had seen abandoned and falling to pieces along Riverside Drive or broken up into apartments like the one his mother lived in.

He scrolled through the pictures without really looking closely and then stopped.

The picture looked to be over a hundred years old, all in shades of brown and tan, showing the house his mother lived in. The words "the Miller House" were scrawled in spidery old-fashioned letters beneath it.

Two tiny figures stood in front of the house: a man and a woman, the man in a bowler hat and the woman in a light-colored dress. Wyatt squinted, trying to see the tiny figures better; the man looked like he could be James. Then again, it could be a rather faded picture of any dark-haired young man.

The woman was pretty, too, younger than the person who might be James, dark-haired like him, not smiling but with a sweet face. Wyatt saved the picture to his computer.

He Googled "19th century Binghamton" this time and came up with more photographs and more brief histories, as well as an academic article entitled "Free Blacks in Nineteenth-Century Binghamton." There was a history of the Endicott Johnson Corporation. Wyatt paged through it, only half paying attention as he tried to figure out if he had enough money in his food budget this week to order takeout again. Really, he should cook. It was both cheaper and better for him. But he felt like Chinese.

Flipping back over to the Binghamton history tab, he backtracked to Google and began to scan the search results. Nothing jumped out at him as particularly interesting, so he closed the tab and went to call in his Chinese order.

Later, with his food spread out across the coffee table, Wyatt put the TV on and sank onto the sofa again.

People in chef's whites were cooking something that looked more expensive than Wyatt's Chinese takeout but not necessarily better tasting. For a moment, he tried to figure out if this was *Top Chef* or *Iron Chef*, possibly *Master Chef*—or *Top Chef Masters*—and then he gave up. They would say what it was eventually, and all four shows were pretty much the same. He pulled his laptop closer and opened it, Googling "Binghamton" again, getting nothing but news articles and links to the university.

He looked from his laptop to the photograph itself. James seemed nothing like what Wyatt would imagine a nineteenth-century bookkeeper would look like, not with his restless intensity. James's shoulders were broad, too, his chest wide beneath his stiff-looking suit. His companion was still a mystery—him with the unreadable eyes. What if they had been queer? What if they'd been trans? Would that change things, and if so, what? Why was it important?

Wyatt rubbed a hand across his face. He wished he could set it aside as easily as Grayson seemed to be able to, but it had lodged somewhere inside of him, this photograph, and it refused to shake loose.

The takeout was getting cold. He stood and gathered it up. He didn't have any major projects, so unless something came up he could swing by the library on his way home and check out the books on Binghamton history. Maybe they'd have something interesting, although he doubted it would be anything Grayson hadn't found. Grayson had probably read all the histories of Binghamton, since that was his job.

He yawned and went back to the living room for his wine bottle and to turn off the TV.

Time to go to bed. He could think about the photograph and legal research tomorrow.

It was snowing again and almost completely dark by the time he got off work and shuffled across the street to the parking garage.

Luckily, the Binghamton Public Library was open until eight, all lit up with bright cheerful lights and almost empty. He gave the librarian sitting behind the front desk his most friendly smile. She glared back at him as he dug out the paper he'd written the names of the books and their call numbers on.

The history section was in a part of the library he'd never been to before. In fact, the whole nonfiction part looked pretty unfamiliar. Wyatt squinted at the spines of the books as he walked through the aisles. Fiction was more his speed. At least, it had been back when he'd read a lot. When he'd been a kid and in college, he'd read mysteries, historical fiction, science fiction, some fantasy. These days, between being the only paralegal under Judge Mayer, watching out for his mother, and helping out Jess whenever she needed it, reality TV took almost too much intellectual energy and commitment.

The section was mostly books about real-life crime and biographies of serial killers, which just seemed gross to Wyatt. He knelt down at the end of the row, hoping there would be more interesting things in the local history section. He ran his fingers down the line of books until he found the ones he was looking for. They all looked old, hardcovered and a little bit deadly. Or very deadly, he thought, pulling one out and seeing it had been written in 1956. Even though it had been made sturdy, the way old books usually were, the cover was starting to break away from the five hundred or so pages contained within. *Going to be slow going with this one.*

He pulled out another volume, knocking a tiny pamphletlike book that was stuck between them to the ground. He picked it up and read the title: *Hauntings and Ghost Stories of Broome County.* It looked fun, at least, so he added it to the stack and carried the armful up to the front desk.

"Excuse me." He coughed, and the librarian transferred her glare from the computer screen to Wyatt's face.

"Yes?"

"I want to check these out." He pushed the books across the counter.

"Do you have a card? You can't check them out without a card." She gave him a once-over as if she doubted someone like him would own a library card or even know what one was. It felt odd to Wyatt, who had always thought he looked like the blandest possible late-twenties-to-early-thirties, office-job-having white dude in his work clothes. Though probably not a whole lot of office-job-having thirty-somethings frequented public libraries in this age of Wikipedia.

He smiled at her anyway and offered her his library card. "Please."

She inspected it carefully, as if someone might actually try to counterfeit a library card. Seeing that it was real, though, she was forced to check out his books for him.

"Thank you." He collected them up along with his card, wishing he'd thought to bring a bag. Seeing as he hadn't, it was a small battle to get the glass doors of the library open without dropping his books on the floor. Somehow he managed, though, and staggered through the parking lot to his car. He stacked them on the roof and dug his keys out before dumping them onto the back seat.

Definitely needed to bring a bag with him next time. He slid into the driver's seat. Maybe he could order Indian on the way. He'd pretty much be going right by there, after all.

Twenty minutes later, Wyatt pushed open the door to his apartment and carried in an armful of books and a plastic shopping bag of takeout Indian food.

He dumped the takeout on the coffee table and went back for the rest of the books. The snow was coming down hard. Wet and thick, it would stick to the ground and accumulate. Driving to work tomorrow would be a treat.

He dialed his mother and sat on the couch playing with the plastic handles of the shopping bag as he listened to it ring. She didn't answer. The answering machine clicked on after several seconds.

It didn't necessarily mean anything was wrong. Sometimes she didn't hear the phone. Some days she was too far gone to remember she had one.

He grabbed his car keys on the way out the door.

She opened the door when he knocked.

"Wyatt, you didn't say you were coming over?"

"Just here to make sure you're okay." He hunched forward, trying to ward off the cold that had seeped into the front hall. "You didn't answer when I called."

It sounded pathetic and overprotective now that he said it out loud.

"I'm sorry." She gave him a fond smile far too similar to ones he remembered from when he'd been young. "I had book group today, and then I was making myself a late dinner. I must have not heard it."

"Yeah." He shifted a little, hands still stuck in his pockets for warmth.

"You want to come in?" She held the door open for him. "I can make enough for two."

"I would love to, but I already ordered out."

She gave him another fond smile. "Then go back home and eat your dinner, and don't worry about me so much. I'm fine."

No, he thought, *you have Alzheimer's disease, you'll never be fine again, and one day you won't even remember who I am.*

"Okay, Mom." He bent down enough to hug her, worried by how thin she felt against him. "I love you."

"I love you, too." She hugged him back with almost as much strength as she'd had when she'd been well, run an entire farm, and raised two kids all by herself. "Really, you don't need to worry."

"Yeah." He held on to her as tightly as he could, but finally he had to pull away. "I'll see you." He waved. "Remember to answer when I call, or call me back, okay?"

"All right." She waved back, looking amused and far too aware.

The takeout was cold by the time he got home, so as far as Wyatt was concerned there was no rush to eat it. He changed into pajama pants and a T-shirt, microwaved himself a plate of food, and got a beer out of the fridge.

He sat on the couch and debated between reading a huge fifty-year-old history of Western New York or watching *Say Yes to the Dress*.

Of course *Say Yes to the Dress* won out, but Wyatt figured he might as well page through the book on local ghost stories while he watched.

There was an entire chapter on the old New York State Inebriate Asylum. The "castle on the hill," as he'd grown up calling it, built in high Gothic fashion in the late nineteenth century. Wyatt found the abandoned asylum incredibly creepy, but there was very little actual ghost lore about it apart from its having once been a Victorian mental asylum. The story of the Victorian house with the floating ghostly heads was much better and a lot creepier.

The last chapter was on the Binghamton Spiritualist Society, formed in 1902. He flipped a page and found a large photograph of three people sitting around a table: two pretty young women in long fancy dresses and a man.

Wyatt stared, then set aside his beer and stared a little bit more. Finally, he put aside the book and went in search of the photograph. It was on his desk. He carried it back to the book of ghost stories. Only when he set the two images side by side was he sure.

"Fuck."

CHAPTER 4

rayson woke to find a text message from Steve. *Girls want to see you, come over for dinner?*

Sure, he texted, and went to take a shower and get ready for work.

He felt the phone vibrate against his leg with an incoming text as he navigated the roads between his house and the Windsor Historical Society. He waited until he was parked before pulling it out.

Next Saturday? Steve had asked. *Girls want to make meatloaf because they say it's your favorite.*

It wasn't. Grayson was a recently ex-vegetarian. But the girls loved making meatloaf, especially with their dad.

Next Saturday's fine, he wrote back. *Meatloaf would be good.* Seeing his nieces again would be excellent, too. He slid out of his car and slogged through the snow toward the historical society door, already feeling pleased about it.

Of course, nothing happened all day long. He filled out and cataloged index cards, wrote up several local history articles for the newsletter, dusted the displays.

There were no genealogists, no local history buffs, not even a random passerby who'd gotten lost.

Grayson wished he could go on Facebook or play a game like a normal person, but the very idea of slacking off while at work made his stomach cramp with anxiety. He formatted the newsletter instead and tried to figure out where to put the giant hundred-and-twenty-year-old taxidermied brown bear that had just been gifted to them.

Five o'clock rolled around, and Grayson figured he might as well lock up and go home.

The door slammed open. He flailed in fright, knocking off his headphones and sending his desk chair skittering backward.

"Jesus Christ!" Grayson spun to see Wyatt coming toward him at a fast trot. He was dressed as he'd been the first time they'd met, right down to the coat and leather satchel. He looked pleased with himself.

"I have something to you show you, something cool."

"Like what?" Grayson retrieved his headphones and put them back on the desk, then turned off the music on his computer before he faced Wyatt.

"Who the second man was." Wyatt rummaged through his bag and came up with the photograph he'd originally brought in, as well as a slim book with a sticky tab marking one of the pages. He thrust both at Grayson. "Take a look."

The sticky tab marked a photograph of two women and a man, all white, all young, wearing clothes that indicated they were middle-class or posing as such. He compared the two photographs and saw what it was Wyatt had seen. "It's the same man."

"Yeah." Grinning, Wyatt perched on the edge of Grayson's desk. "It turns out this was one of the founding members of the Binghamton Spiritualist Society. His name was Liam Devlin."

"This is amazing." Grayson flipped through the chapter, but there was nothing else about Liam Devlin except for his name in the caption of the photograph. "I can't believe you found this."

Wyatt beamed at him. He leaned over to read the page as well, bringing them very close together. Close enough that their shoulders brushed.

"Do you think this is how they met? Something to do with this?" Wyatt bent closer, and Grayson went completely rigid.

"Impossible to tell."

"But it could be." Grayson pushed his chair back the inch or so it took to give them both a little bit of space.

When he looked up, Wyatt was watching him with a pensive expression. "You know, when I look at the photograph, I see this ..." He bit his lip, his gaze searching for something in Grayson's expression. "This kinship. I can look at them and see myself there. There's an intimacy here, to me, the way they relate to each other, their closeness, and the stillness in this moment. I know you don't feel that. I know that's not how you value or judge these things, but it's what I see."

Wyatt had gone a little pink as he spoke, cheeks flushing. Grayson didn't know what to say. For a moment, their gazes caught and held, but then Wyatt looked away.

"I mean, that might sound stupid—" Wyatt began, and Grayson's whole body rejected what would come after.

"No," he interrupted. "I don't think it's stupid at all." He needed Wyatt to understand, and he found himself gripping Wyatt's arm before he could stop himself. "You're right, I don't know if I see what you do, but I am still interested in these two."

He let go of Wyatt's arm and looked back down at the book on the desk.

"Thank you." Wyatt had shifted a little bit closer, but Grayson didn't let himself look up.

"I didn't know there was a Binghamton Spiritualist Society. I mean, I'm not surprised, really."

"Why not surprised?" Wyatt leaned against the desk again, his hand right alongside Grayson's.

"Well, this is Upstate New York." The joke settled him a little, and he looked up, grinning, but Wyatt's expression was blank. "Burned-over district? Lily Dale? The Oneida Community?" He deflated when Wyatt just kept staring. "Mormonism?"

"Okay, that last one I know. But what does this have to do with Mormonism?"

"Mormonism was founded in Upstate New York. The Oneida Community was a religious commune started in 1848 in Oneida, New York, that practiced polygamy, among other things. The burned-over district was a nickname for the entirety of Upstate New York during the nineteenth century because of all the religious revivals and cults that formed here, and Lily Dale is an entire town founded on spiritualism in the early twentieth century and populated almost exclusively by mediums."

"An entire town?" Wyatt looked intrigued now.

"It was a small town, but yeah, spiritualism was big here, to say the least."

Wyatt's smile widened into a grin.

Grayson raised his eyebrows. "What?"

"Nothing." Wyatt actually straight-up laughed, and it was amazing the way it made him light up, his face becoming rounder, younger, his eyes coming to life.

Grayson looked down at his hands twisted together in his lap. "What?"

"To say the least? Who says that?"

That made Grayson look up, but there wasn't any mockery about the smile Wyatt gave him. It was sweet, really, and Grayson was very aware they weren't that far apart now, not at all, almost close enough to touch.

"Well, I would hope *I* talk like that. After all the money I spent getting educated? If I didn't talk like I was in a costume drama, I'd probably ask for refund."

Not a good joke, but Wyatt didn't stop smiling. "I like it."

It made Grayson so warm and unsure of what to do with his hands.

"Do you want to get a drink with me?" A tentativeness crept into Wyatt's voice as he asked, his smile fading a little.

"Like a date?"

"Yes, like a date." Wyatt had gone all uncertain, looking at the floor.

"Okay." Grayson reached out before he could think better of it. He let his hand rest over Wyatt's just for a moment.

Wyatt was smiling again when he looked up at Grayson. "Good. Do you want to do that now, or do you have something else planned for tonight?"

"No." Grayson shook his head, didn't give himself time to think maybe that sounded pathetic. "Tonight works for me."

"Okay, so do you know where the Lost Dog is?" Wyatt pulled out his phone, probably to check if it was open and if they needed reservations.

"Yeah." Grayson had never been there, but he knew where it was.

Wyatt nodded, then hesitated. "Would you rather grab dinner actually? I know drinks are generally considered a cooler choice, but I'm actually hungry."

"Yeah, so am I."

"So is Lost Dog still okay?" Wyatt looked a little unsure, probably because the Lost Dog was the most expensive restaurant in town.

"Little Venice?" Grayson offered. It was in the same general area as Lost Dog but a lot cheaper.

"Lost Dog might be better, you know." Wyatt made a small, meaningless gesture.

For a same-sex couple, Grayson thought. He meant it would be safer for two men on a date. The idea that he could pass and by passing put himself in danger was a new twist on an old fear. Perfect.

"Yeah, probably the Lost Dog is best."

"Lost Dog it is, then."

The Lost Dog was a cute little brick building not that far from downtown. It had big windows decorated with garlands of lights with a vintage-looking converted industrial interior. It was trying for young and hip and was about as upscale as Binghamton got.

Needless to say, it was almost always packed with university people, but today was a weekday and not terribly late, so Wyatt was indeed able to get them a table.

"Ever been here?" Wyatt asked after Grayson settled himself at their little table and they placed their orders.

"No." It occurred to Grayson that he'd never actually gone on a date while living in Binghamton. High school had been something of a wash romantically and sexually. Then, once he'd come back, he'd been too busy transitioning and alienating everyone he knew by doing so. "It's nice, though."

He sipped the water their server had brought them and eyed Wyatt from under his lashes. Wyatt, he was pretty sure, had not come to the historical society to ask him out. His white dress shirt looked a little rumpled, and his tie was striped with dark gray, light gray, and dark blue lines. It looked like it was polyester or some kind of acrylic blend, horrible in its own right. Remembering the skinny jeans and oversized sweater combo, Grayson was pretty sure this was not how Wyatt would choose to dress on a date.

So it had been a spur-of-the-moment thing. Brought on by how devastatingly sexy Grayson was lecturing on late-nineteenth-century spiritualism? He doubted it. But then, what? As far as he could tell, all they shared in common was being queer and being interested in two men who'd probably died at least sixty years ago, and who might or might not have been a couple.

You said yes, didn't you? He had. And watching Wyatt frown at the menu, or more likely the prices, he wasn't sorry.

"Do you come here a lot?" Grayson guessed that was a no even before Wyatt shook his head.

"Last time I was here was when my sister got engaged."

Grayson thought of his own sister, whom he hadn't spoken to in years. "So what do you do for a living? We talk about my work but not yours."

"I work as a paralegal down at the courthouse." Wyatt took a sip of water, looking a little pensive. "But I can't talk about a lot of it for confidentiality reasons."

"Gotcha. Okay, then." Grayson had a vague idea that paralegals assisted lawyers in some way, but did that make them more like lawyers who special-ized or like administrative assistants? He watched

Wyatt, trying to decide if Wyatt looked like he'd gone to law school. Law school was three years on top of a four-year degree, right? Wyatt looked to be about Grayson's age, which meant he totally could have done that and then been working for a couple of years at least.

"You're from Binghamton?" The subject was more neutral than Wyatt's work, hopefully. He really didn't want to go back to talking about himself.

"Well, kind of. I grew up out where you live now, actually, past Windsor. We owned a farm out there."

"Oh, yeah?" Not all that surprising; the area around Binghamton had always been small family farms, mostly. Some of them supplied "local" vegetables to New York City, just as they had for the past two hundred years. He hadn't pegged Wyatt for a farmer, though.

"My mom doesn't run it anymore, obviously. Our farmhand and his family run it now. They're great people."

"Your mom's not up for it anymore?"

"No."

The way Wyatt stiffened made Grayson hesitant to ask further about his life.

Their server came bearing food, and there was a moment of silence as they moved glasses and silverware out of the way to make room for the plates, then began eating.

"So what do you do when you're not doing history?" Wyatt asked.

He was toying with his fork. Grayson was becoming increasingly aware that he was stuffing his face while Wyatt wasn't eating at all.

"I read." Grayson put his own fork down. "I read a lot of different kinds of novels along with nonfiction in my spare time." He searched for something else to say about that, maybe some way to make him sound less boring. Unfortunately, that would probably take an act of God, and God didn't seem to be eating at the Lost Dog tonight. "What kind of books do you like to read?"

Wyatt looked down at the fish all laid out nicely on the plate with a little bit of sauce and garnish. "I don't read all that often anymore."

"Oh." *Well, good, put your foot in it*, Grayson thought. *Save it, save it before it sinks.* He'd had these kinds of dates, the kind where he said something stupid or overly academic and it just tanked the entire endeavor. "I watch TV, too," he offered. "*Star Trek, X-Files ...*" *Good. Great. Way to sound like the world's biggest geek.* He gave Wyatt a tense smile. This was why he hated dating. Sex good. Relationships great. But the awkward dating stage sucked.

"I liked *The X-Files* when it was on TV the first time." Wyatt leaned forward a little bit, not seeming that put off, which was a good sign. "I've not seen it since, though. Might be fun to rewatch."

"Yeah, I've been enjoying it." Grayson congratulated himself for at least not having bombed that one.

Wyatt scooped up a bite and, to Grayson's relief, ate it.

"So what do you do when you're not working or researching local history?" Grayson asked.

"Much like you, I watch TV. I'm still close to a bunch of the people I went to college with, and we hang out."

Grayson had hated everyone he'd known in high school, and all the people he'd gone to college and then graduate school with either lived in New York City or in another state. "That sounds like fun."

They stared at each other, the awkward silence hanging between them like a tiny dark cloud. Grayson began to have a bad feeling about the outcome of this date.

"So." Grayson reached for the only topic they seemed to have in common. "What makes you think James and Liam were a couple?"

"I don't know, it was just a feeling. I was looking at them and the way they were sitting." He shrugged. "It just seemed like there was something there. Not to mention they'd be cute. They're both kind of good-looking."

"Yeah, they are."

The conversation lapsed again, and Grayson concentrated on eating his pasta. Wyatt ate the rest of his fish, and the servers came for the plates.

"We can split it." Grayson reached for his wallet as he spoke.

Wyatt opened his mouth, then closed it. "Sure. All right."

When the bill came, Grayson laid down half along with a generous tip, and Wyatt covered the rest of it.

When they'd both gotten their coats on, they walked outside together.

He knew it was coming. He braced himself for it as they stepped into the chill night air and walked along the sidewalk toward the parking garage. A small group of boisterous university students bumped past them. One of the guys had his arm around a young woman's waist.

Both Grayson and Wyatt slowed their pace to walk behind the group, which seemed to be heading for the parking garage or the student apartments nearby.

The group stopped to cross the street. The yellow glow of a streetlight cast strange shadows. Grayson watched the young man's hand drift from the girl's shoulder to rest on her ass.

"Greg!" She batted his hand away and then giggled, leaning into him harder. Greg grinned back, completely without remorse, and replaced his hand.

"Stop." She grabbed his wrist this time, glanced behind them at Grayson and Wyatt, and then leaned close to Greg's ear. "There are people watching."

She spoke in the loudest stage whisper Grayson had ever heard.

"So?" Greg whispered back just as loud. "Let them."

The girl laughed again and draped herself across part of Greg's chest, leaning heavily on his shoulder, face buried in the curve of his neck as she continued to giggle hysterically. Greg laughed along with her, arms around her waist.

They were drunk, Grayson thought, or just very young. He stuffed his hands in his coat pockets and waited for the light to change. Wyatt was silent beside him, also waiting.

The light changed. The group surged across the street.

Grayson concentrated on the pavement, the city around him, and Wyatt beside him. He tried not to think about the kids.

Ahead of them, Greg and the girl had stopped. They kissed as their friends yelled at them, *Hurry up!* and *Stop being gross, you two!*

Grayson and Wyatt edged around them and crossed the street to the parking garage.

They'd parked on the second floor. Grayson climbed the stairs in silence.

It's not going to work out, Grayson told himself as they crossed the dark space to their cars. *You are not going to get upset about it, you're just going to accept that's the way it is. Things like this don't always work out. You've been on enough failed dates to know that.*

Wyatt stopped next to his car and turned to Grayson. "Tonight was great."

Grayson held himself still and stiff. Wyatt wasn't touching him, wasn't even looking at him.

"I enjoyed myself, too." It was almost entirely a lie, but Grayson didn't know what else to say.

"We should do it again." Wyatt still wouldn't look at him. "Sometime."

"Sometime," Grayson echoed back, a polite formality.

Look at me, he thought with all the force he could muster. *Look at me.*

"Great." Wyatt dug out his car keys and finally looked at Grayson with eyes that said, *I'm sorry, I'm so sorry.* He gave Grayson a tight little smile. "Thank you."

"Hey, no problem." All Grayson could think about was how much he wanted the ground to open up and suck him right through the floor of the parking garage.

Why had he thought this was actually going to happen?

"I'll see you later." The words hung in his ears, sounding desperate and pathetic. Grayson's fingers felt numb closed around his car keys.

Wyatt didn't answer, didn't turn around, just got in his car and started the engine. Grayson would not let himself watch Wyatt drive away, or, more accurately, would not let Wyatt see him watching him drive away.

There were certain levels he would not stoop to, he would not ... his hands shook so badly, he fumbled the keys trying to unlock the door to his car. Tears pricked at the corners of his eyes, and Grayson clenched his teeth until his jaw ached. *You will not cry*, he told himself over and over again. *Do not dare cry, you pathetic little* ... He jerked the door open and climbed into the driver's seat, clenched his hands around the wheel trying to stop them from shaking. He had to get all the way out to Windsor tonight without killing himself, after all. Closing his eyes, he tried to think of something else—his nieces laughing hysterically as he took turns spinning them around, calling him "Uncle Grayson" and clinging to his legs as he cooked dinner.

Eventually, his hands stopped shaking, his breathing calmed, and the desire to cry lessened.

It was a bad date.

Grayson started the car and let it warm before backing out of the parking space.

Bad dates happened, and he hadn't really thought he'd ever date Wyatt anyway. He was an idiot for getting this upset about Wyatt—about a spur-of-the-minute date Wyatt had obviously regretted asking him on.

It was a good twenty minutes from downtown Binghamton to his house. The fields surrounding the road were dark, his own house shut up and uninviting.

No one is going to love you, his mother had told him with tears running down her face, her makeup smeared into long, dark stains across her cheeks. *If you ruin yourself like this, no one will ever love you again.*

Grayson banged his hands as hard as he could against the steering wheel. He kept hitting until his palms were red from it. It had been a stupid date, one stupid date, he'd messed up dates before. It had nothing to do with his identity. It didn't have to do with anything except bad luck.

He knew that.

Knowing didn't change anything at all.

He climbed out of the car and trekked toward the house. Bed was the best option right now.

Tomorrow, he could start pretending like this had never happened.

CHAPTER 5

The alarm on his cell phone went off, his phone vibrating across his bedside table. Wyatt reached for it, flicked it off, and tossed it onto the other side of the bed.

He hadn't slept.

It was Saturday, so no work, but he'd promised Jess he'd come over. He rolled out of bed and went to find himself some coffee.

In the kitchen, he tripped over a pile of tiles and grabbed the edge of the counter before he face-planted into it.

"Fuck!" His foot hurt like the worst stubbed toe ever. He pressed his forehead against the cool surface of the counter and wondered if he could just go back to bed. Instead, he knelt down and examined his foot. It throbbed, but not enough to actually be broken, so Wyatt stood back up and limped to the coffeemaker.

He was stirring sugar into his coffee when the guilt struck him again like a brick to the back of the head. He was an idiot, but also far worse than that.

"You're a dick." Wyatt gave his coffee one last stir and took it into the living room.

He watched his coffee go cold.

Oh, yes. Mixed into his guilt and shame, there was a distinct streak of melodramatic self-pity. And right when he thought he couldn't develop any more unattractive qualities.

Wyatt carried his cold coffee into the kitchen and dumped it in the sink, then went to get dressed.

He put on jeans and a tight-fitting gray cotton shirt with a low-cut neck and long sleeves. On top went a gauzy, bright scarf he hoped he wasn't going to get in trouble for, boots, and his jacket.

Sometimes walking cleared his mind, so Wyatt walked across the bridge to Otsiningo. There were trails there, one that looped around a little artificial pond, another that ran the entire length of the park. Wyatt took the pond trail.

The sun was bright, the sky clear and blue with only wisps of clouds. The air was cold, though. Wyatt's breath hung before him in trails of white.

For the few days the picture of James and Liam had preyed on his mind, he'd even dreamed about it. He couldn't stop thinking about the two of them and how much he still didn't know. It was depressing to think he'd never know more than he did. He could continue to do his own research, but he doubted he'd get very far without Grayson to help.

There he was, back to thinking about Grayson again. Wyatt stopped walking. He scuffed his foot over some dirt on the path. God, he didn't want to think about Grayson. It was actually physically painful. Even though he was trying not to, his mind would catch on the memory of the way Grayson had looked when they'd said good night. Wyatt's body would ache, hot pain starting in his chest and spreading through him, into his bones. There was so much guilt and shame, like a cloud in his mind waiting to consume his thoughts and make him heavy with misery.

He started walking again, this time faster, really stretching his legs and propelling himself down the path. Finally, he turned off the one he'd been walking and started down the longer one.

Trees shaded this path, their branches now bare of leaves. Beyond them, he could just make out the wide gray width of the river.

Hands shoved in his pockets, he looked over the river. It was high now, fat with the melted snow, although not as high as it would be in spring.

He felt tied to James and Liam in a way he'd never been to historical people before.

It was odd, when he stopped to think about it, to never see yourself reflected in history, to have no sense of yourself in time. The idea that you could be linked to others across time and space based on shared experience—it had always seemed like it didn't apply to people like him.

Maybe it could, and maybe it did, and wasn't that at the end of the day what he needed? Yes, he wanted to know everything he could about James and Liam, but more than that—far more—Wyatt wanted to know he wasn't alone.

Did you know?

Wasn't that the question he'd been asking Liam and James since he'd dug them out of that attic? *Did you know what I know? Did you feel this too?*

The question was related to who they had been, obviously, but it was more, too—something bigger. Wyatt wasn't looking for these two people alone, he was looking for all of them—all of the people like him and like Grayson. They weren't supposed to exist in the past, or at least it was a history he'd never come across before. What if they did, though? What if there was a past of people who had been queer and trans, a past that would say, *This is who we are, and this is how we fit into this world.* Would it be easier then?

It mattered to him. That connection he had with the photograph, it meant a lot, feeling connected like that. If he could know in some way that there were others who'd gone through what he'd gone through—not just the ones who were alive now, but people who'd lived their lives long before he was ever born—it would be important. Maybe he wasn't a great historian or academic, and he couldn't articulate why it would be important, but he knew it anyway.

There were moments when he looked at the photograph and wondered why it had been hidden. What it meant to hide a picture like that away. More than just proof of an illicit and interracial affair, it felt so personal the way the photograph had been shot, the lighting, the way they were seated—everything about it. The vulnerability and wariness in both their faces. If it was a picture of him, raw in its guardedness, in its watchfulness and waiting, would he have kept it? He would certainly never have displayed it, he knew that.

But in a lot of ways that was what made this photograph important. It wasn't hypothetical. It was personal.

Wyatt knew what it was to live with his cards permanently close to his chest, to always have a part of him unacknowledged and unseen.

He didn't want a queer past that didn't include that, that was only ever about being out. Because that was what the GLBT community was like far too often: if you weren't out, you didn't exist. It was terrifying and painful.

He wanted to point to this photograph and say, *See? See? I exist, I still exist.*

There were tears in his eyes, but he couldn't cry here at the park surrounded by dog walkers and ducks and fallen leaves.

He thought about Grayson, about calling him and telling him everything he'd been thinking. It felt like possibly falling apart, but he was so tired. Just this once he wanted someone to know. There were tears on his face. Wyatt pulled his gloves off and wiped them away.

A jogger rushed by him on the path, followed by a twenty-something man walking a dog. The dog paused to sniff at him, and the man pulled the dog away with a few words and an apologetic smile.

Wyatt turned from his view of the river and started to walk home.

He'd crashed on the couch after a day of sitting in on hearings when his phone vibrated its way across the coffee table. Wyatt reached for it, mind still on what he was going to order for dinner and if he needed to stop by a liquor store for another bottle of wine.

It was Jess. He unlocked the phone and answered it. "Yeah?"

"It's Mom." Jess's voice had a controlled edge of panic, and Wyatt sat up.

"What's happened?"

"I called her earlier today and we talked, and she was doing bad, drifting, not remembering, she didn't even remember Timothy and I were living together, much less getting married for Christ's sake, and I just tried to call her back and it couldn't get through." Jess took a breath. "I've tried three times, Wyatt."

"It's all right." He already had his car keys in his hand, and he was reaching for his coat. "I'm going over there now, but I'm sure she's fine."

On the other end of the phone, Jess let out a breath. "Thank you. I just worry about her being by herself at this point."

Wyatt's fingers tightened around his phone. "I know. I'll call and let you know what's going on once I get there."

"Thanks."

The line went dead. Wyatt started for his car.

His mother's apartment looked dark from the outside, which was a bad sign this early in the evening. Wyatt took the stairs two at a time and knocked hard on her front door. Nothing happened, so he knocked again. Still no answer. He let himself in with his spare key.

It was completely dark in the apartment. Wyatt began to feel his way through from the kitchen into the living room, turning on lights as he went.

"Wyatt?"

The door to the bedroom opened, and his mother shuffled out. She wore a ratty nightgown. Her gray hair hung free down her back. She squinted at him. "Wyatt, why are you here so late?"

"It's not late." He approached her slowly, carefully. "It's only a little after five p.m."

She blinked at him, not comprehending. "But ..." She turned toward the window, where the sky outside was dark.

"It's almost winter," he told her gently. "It gets dark early now."

She just blinked up at him mutely.

"Mom." He reached out and took her hands in his. "Are you remembering to take your medication?"

"Medication?" The look she gave him was totally blank. "But Wyatt, you know I'm never sick."

He let go of her hands and opened the cupboard where her medication was stored. The plastic sorter felt too heavy as soon as he picked it up. When he flipped open the caps, it became obvious what had happened. Wyatt shut his eyes for a moment and prayed for patience and strength.

"You haven't been taking your medication for a couple days." He held out the container. "You said you were."

She looked from the medication organizer to his face, her expression confused and a little lost.

Wyatt sighed and set it aside. "Come on, have you eaten? Let me cook something."

Still in his work clothes, Wyatt pulled off his tie and rolled up the sleeves of his shirt before starting to look through the refrigerator.

When Jess and Timothy took her shopping, they often cleaned out the fridge as well, so most of the food in there was safe to eat. There was some chicken that looked all right and a carton of premade soup. He pulled both out and began finding pots and pans.

"You don't have to cook." She came across the kitchen to stand beside him. "I can do that." She reached for the pan, but Wyatt moved it out of her grasp.

"No, it's all right, let me."

"No." Her voice grew hard. Wyatt moved the frying pan even farther way.

"Mom." He took her by the arm and guided her to a chair by the table. "I would love for you to cook dinner for me sometime, but not tonight. I want to cook dinner tonight, okay?"

"All right." She sat at the table looking tired and a lot older than she should have.

"Let me just start the chicken." Wyatt turned back to the stove, stamping hard on the panic rising in his chest. He needed to call Jess, needed to talk to her about this, but dinner and making sure his mother got to bed came first.

She sat at the kitchen table and watched him as he reheated the soup. Wyatt kept trying to think of something to say, some way of lightening the mood, but nothing seemed appropriate. If Jess had been there, she would have said or done something to put them all at ease. Everything Wyatt thought of stuck in his throat. He poured the soup into bowls and brought them both over to the table, along with her medicine and a glass of water.

They ate in silence until Wyatt finally forced himself to fill the space between them with chatter about how he thought he might get vacation time soon and how one of the administrative assistants was expecting a baby and he needed to think of a good gift. What he wanted to say remained caught behind his teeth.

"Why don't you go sit in the other room while I do the dishes?" He turned her gently toward the living room and watched her go before tackling the cleanup.

He tried to clear his mind as he washed, concentrating only on the mechanics of rubbing the dishes with the sponge, rinsing, and rubbing again. Anxiety filled his throat like acid, made his stomach heave like he was going to be sick. His face felt hot, tears lurking just behind his eyes. The last dish went into the drainer a little harder than he'd meant. For a moment, he stood still, eyes closed, breathing deeply.

Then he wiped his hands off on his slacks and turned toward the living room.

She was curled up on the couch, lit by a warm yellow glow from the lamps on the side tables.

"Wyatt?" She looked up at him when he entered. "Are you angry at me?"

"No, I ... no." Wyatt sat beside her on the couch. "We just need to be more careful to make sure you get your medication, okay? You can't skip again."

She nodded, but without any real comprehension, and bit her lip.

They were quiet for a moment where they sat, shoulders just touching. Wyatt wanted to lean into her and have her hug him like she used to when he'd been a kid upset over something that had happened at school.

"I messed up," he found himself saying, looking down at his hands. "I went on a date, it's been almost two weeks ago now, and I ..." He took a long, deep breath. "And I acted in a way I'm not proud of."

Her hand touched his, and he looked up at her.

"You're seeing someone new?" Her brow furrowed a little bit.

"I was." He took her hand in his, held on tight. "The thing is, I really liked him. He's cute and a good person and so smart. He has a graduate degree, you know, and I don't know why he even agreed to go out with someone like me."

"Probably because you're cute and smart and a good person, too." His mother sounded dry and sharp, more like herself now, and Wyatt looked up to find her smiling at him. His eyes filled with tears as he leaned forward to hug her tight. She felt so frail against him, but she still hugged him back. "Oh, Wyatt, love, did you do or say something to hurt him?"

Wyatt took a long, shuddering breath. The shame crawled under his skin and leached into his chest, icy cold and painful. The worst part, far worse than being stupid, was that he'd been a coward, and also unkind.

"I did hurt him." His voice came out very quiet. "I didn't mean to, but I ..." How much should he say here, how much *could* he say?

Here on the couch together, with her still hugging him tight, he wanted to tell her everything. He wanted to say, *I'm not a boy, Mom, I'm trans and I've known for a long time. Please, please still love me.*

The words stuck in his throat, though, settling cold and hard like metal inside of him. It was like being at the restaurant with Grayson all over again. He'd known he needed to come out to Grayson, but just the idea had started his hands shaking. What would Grayson say? Would he believe Wyatt? What if he didn't? What would happen if Grayson didn't want to have anything to do with him because Wyatt was in the closet, or because Wyatt was genderqueer?

Or what if Grayson had second thoughts because Wyatt was assigned male at birth?

What if he came out now to his mother and she … stopped loving him? He could tell himself as much as he wanted that she wouldn't, but what if she did? Parents reacted badly to their kids coming out as trans all the time—hated them for it, even.

It was like having a panic attack in slow motion. His chest contracted painfully, his breathing coming fast and labored.

"Hey." She pulled back and looked at him. "There now. Don't get upset. Whatever you did, it can't be that bad. I know you."

But you don't, not all of me.

He forced a smile for her and concentrated on breathing through the panic. She rubbed his shoulder soothingly. He couldn't come out, but he could risk telling her some of it, surely.

He took another calming breath and sat back so he could see her face. "He's trans, Mom."

He watched her expression change too quickly for him to really be sure of.

"So he was born a girl?" His heart sank just a tiny bit.

"Assigned female at birth," he corrected. She thought about this for a moment.

"And that upset you?" she asked at last. "Or did you say something offensive to him about it?"

He couldn't help but cringe. "God, I hope not."

"So what did you do, sweetie?" She took his hand again.

"I freaked out halfway through, I thought he'd judge me. I thought it would be different somehow." *Because I'm trans too, and I didn't have the guts to say that—can't say it now.* "I know it wouldn't be, not really, it could be good, better even than other relationships I've had, but I got scared and I froze up. I think he thought I was rejecting him." He put his head down. "Because I was. I did reject him."

There was a long silence.

"But now you wish you hadn't," his mother said finally, and Wyatt's head came up.

"Yeah. I wish I hadn't done any of it, really."

She patted his hand. "We can't change what we've already done, but if you want to go out with this"— she hesitated for just a second—"young man, you need to apologize and hope it's enough for him to forgive you. But if he doesn't, then he doesn't."

He ducked his head. "I know."

"You'll find someone. If not this young man, then someone else, someone you can be happy with." Her tone was confident, as always. She'd encouraged him and Jess to date without being serious about it when they were younger. As he'd gotten older, though, she'd made no secret of wanting to see him in a long-term relationship. He didn't blame her. He wanted that, too.

He squeezed her hand. "I hope so."

They lapsed into silence. She started to fidget, pulling her hand free, and then sighed. When he looked over, she was drifting a little bit again, losing that sharp focus she'd been forcing in order to listen to him. She must be getting tired; it was late, after all.

"Do you want to watch something?" he asked. "You want to watch *Say Yes to the Dress*?"

"All right." She seemed almost relieved, shifting beside him to turn toward the television.

They worked their way through the episode about having too many people in the bridal party and then the episode about brides who'd changed their minds about their wedding dresses. Wyatt tried to concentrate on the show. The palms of his hands itched with tension. He wanted to leap up and pace.

Finally, she yawned, and he hit pause and turned to her. "Do you want to continue watching or go to bed?"

She blinked at him. He touched her arm. "Want to go to bed now, Mom?"

"Yes." She stood, smoothing down her nightgown.

"Do you need anything to go to bed with? Your reading glasses, a glass of water?"

"Yes, I"—she patted down her nightgown as if looking for pockets that weren't there—"don't know where my glasses are."

"Come on." He led the way to the bedroom, turning on the lights as they went. There was a mystery novel open on the bedside table, but it had a thin layer of dust on it. "Well, your book is here." He dusted it off and handed it to her. She squinted at the title as if she'd never seen it before.

"I was reading this?"

"I'm assuming so." He searched around the bedside table and then opened the drawer, finally locating her glasses.

"Here." After setting the glasses on the bedside table, he straightened the covers like she used to do for him when he was little.

She climbed into the bed, settled the book on her lap, and reached for her glasses.

"You okay? Need anything else?"

"I'm fine." She gave him a smile and put her glasses on, opening the book to the first page again.

"Okay. Good night, Mom. I love you."

"I love you, too." She reached up to pull him down into a quick hug. "And I'm very proud of you."

He hugged her back hard. "Get some sleep. I'll see you tomorrow, okay?"

"Okay." She was smiling when he headed out of the room, leaving her to her book and hopefully some rest.

He let himself out of the bedroom and pulled out his cell phone to speed-dial Jess. It rang only once before she answered. "What's happening? Is Mom okay?"

"She hasn't been taking her medication." He paced the room. "She hasn't been taking it for days, so of course when I got here she was a mess. I got her calmed down and back on track, I think. We even had a conversation once she'd taken her meds, but this is bad."

"She said she was." Jess sounded as tired and frustrated as he felt. "Last time I was over I asked, and she told me that she'd been taking her meds."

"Yeah, she told me the same thing." Wyatt rubbed his fingers through his hair.

"Well, the doctor did say she would start lying and making things up. It would get to a point where we couldn't believe everything she said. The disease warps her memories as well as takes them away."

Wyatt sat on the couch and let his head drop into his hand. "We need to start looking into assisted living. If she can't remember to take her meds, she can't live alone."

"Yeah."

There was a long silence as they both thought of what that would mean.

"I don't trust any of them here." Wyatt pressed his hand against his mouth and then let it drop to his side. "We could try and get her into the one up in Ithaca, though."

"It's so expensive."

"Yeah. But I could—" Wyatt closed his eyes. "I could move. In a smaller place I would need less rent, and the rest could go to paying for her to be there. We could look into selling the farm. We'll probably need to anyway, as a long-term plan. I'm just worried about where to get the money short-term."

"Timothy and I have set aside money for the wedding. We could use that for the down payment to secure her a space and put off getting married another year."

"Is Timothy going to go for that?" Wyatt knew they'd been saving for years. To take that money and put it toward something else was huge.

Jess sighed. "I'll talk to him about it."

"I don't want that for you. You and Timothy have waited long enough. You deserve a nice wedding."

"But Mom deserves someplace safe to live more."

Wyatt didn't have much to say to that. Jess was right. And he couldn't imagine where else the money could come from. "Yeah. We can look into homes for Mom? Maybe we'll find someplace less expensive that'll be nice and safe for her. Until then, one of us is going to have to stop by every morning to make sure she's taking her medication."

"Okay. Timothy and I can probably take most weekdays if you'll handle the weekends. That way, you won't have to worry about it before work, and I won't have to worry about it on my two busiest days of the week."

"Thank you, and thank Timothy for me, too. It would be great if you could just check and make sure she's doing okay during the week. And I'll try to spend more evenings over here, too." There really wasn't a whole lot else they could do.

"We can meet and talk about this. I'm just glad she was okay tonight. And thanks for going over there and taking care of her."

"Of course. I'll always be there for Mom." He really wanted to hug her. Having someone to hold and lean against right now would be perfect.

"Take care of yourself, too." Jess sounded genuinely concerned. Wyatt laughed, although without a whole lot of humor.

"Yeah. Take care, Jess."

"You too, sweetie."

The phone went dead against his ear. Wyatt set it aside and put his head in his hands.

What were they going to do? What were they going to *do*? She would only get worse, never better, and they'd known when they moved her into this apartment that she would only be able to survive on her own for a short time. He'd hoped and prayed they'd have more time than this, though.

Feeling helpless was easy in situations like this, but it wouldn't get them anywhere. The dementia was progressing. That was just a fact. It affected everyone differently. It was also unpredictable, making it impossible to guess a few months ago where she'd be now.

Knowing all of that didn't make it less scary, but being afraid wasn't going to change this, either.

He took several deep breaths and let himself lean back against the couch.

After he felt calmer, he got up and collected his keys, heading for his car. Anxiety and fatigue were making his whole body hurt.

He kicked off his shoes as soon as he got into the apartment and collapsed on the couch. What he needed to do was go to bed, but he was still a little bit too tightly wound to sleep. Soon, though, because exhaustion was starting to bleed through the edges of his nervous energy. Wyatt pressed a hand against his eyes and considered making himself a drink to see if it calmed him. Instead, he let his gaze drift around the room, coming to rest on the photograph on the coffee table.

Leaning forward, he rested his elbows on his knees and looked down at James and Liam. He reached for the closeness, the connection he knew was there, but tonight he couldn't feel it. He rubbed a hand over his eyes and looked at the floor.

When he'd told Grayson about the photograph, Grayson hadn't brushed it off or told him he was wrong. He might not have seen it, but he'd believed that Wyatt had.

Wyatt's only higher education was two years of community college. He lived in the same town he'd grown up in, having never gone anywhere else. He'd only been to New York City once, and that was on a school field trip when he'd been twelve. He worked as a glorified administrative assistant. The only job he'd had before that was two years working part-time at Taco Bell. There was no reason on earth for Grayson to treat him like an equal, and yet Grayson did.

He remembered the way Grayson had looked when he'd been lecturing Wyatt about New York history. He'd exuded confidence, an unshakable knowledge that he was right underpinning every word. His hands moved when he talked, illustrating his speech, and his eyes crinkled when he smiled, his entire being coming to life with power and light.

He was fire when he smiled, all heat and uncountable energy, lightning when he spoke. Grayson had showed him that passion. He didn't dumb down things, didn't leave out details because he thought Wyatt wouldn't be able to understand.

It made Wyatt want call him up and beg for another chance. He hadn't been ready to come out to Grayson before, and he might never be ready to come out to his mother, but he wanted to tell Grayson now. He wanted to know what it would be like to say, "I'm trans" out loud to someone. Whether Grayson would give him a chance to repair what he'd messed up, he didn't know. He wanted to try, though. Because if Grayson did give him another chance and Wyatt did come out, it would be the first relationship he'd ever been in where he could be completely open, whole for the first time. He wanted that so much, wanted Grayson's passion and confidence. He wanted to be called by pronouns he chose and to be seen, really seen, for the first time in his life.

Tomorrow, he'd do research into assisted-living facilities for his mother.

Then he'd call Grayson.

CHAPTER 6

Grayson stared at the computer screen without seeing it. He'd been doing intake cataloging for the new stuff, but it was starting to blur together now. All day, he'd been trying to find tasks around the office to distract himself with. Usually, he was happy to do anything related to history, no matter how small or seemingly pointless. Nothing held his attention today, though. It irritated him.

What he needed was a research project. He could work on his master's thesis—the one his advisor had told him should be expanded as the basis for his dissertation. Just thinking about that made panic rise, though. Made him feel like a failure.

So maybe not that research exactly. He'd have to find a new project to work on. Or he could work on the photograph again.

He pressed his hands against his eyes. The last thing he wanted to do was think about Wyatt and the whole debacle. But the actual research might be interesting.

If Liam was a medium or at least involved in the spiritualist movement, that information might help track him down. One of Grayson's cohort from grad school, Rachel, had done research on nineteenth-century spiritualism, hadn't she? He pushed himself back to the computer and opened up his browser to write her an email. She might have some resources for him, archives or people he could contact.

He shot off the message.

Where else could he look? He drummed his fingers on the table. Well, he could still access newspapers like the *New York Times* and some local ones. Even mediums had to advertise. Also, he should check out all the books he could find about spiritualism in the United States. Even if they didn't mention Liam, it would be good to have that background information. Wyatt had originally found Liam in a local history book, so Grayson should check all of those out, too. Liam couldn't have been that famous or prominent within the spiritualist movement if there was this little information on him. Perhaps he had dabbled or had been a medium on the side. He would have been practicing his 'craft' during the later period of spiritualism. Grayson had a vague idea Houdini had been disproving famous mediums at the time, and people were turning a bit more skeptical. If Liam hadn't been able to do it full-time or had been an amateur, that could make tracking him down even more difficult, since his ties to the spiritualist community would be fewer.

Grayson rubbed his forehead. Maybe he should call up the Binghamton Historical Society and see if they had a list of local histories, or recommendations at least. It would give him somewhere to start, and it wouldn't hurt him in this job to have more background in local history.

When he glanced at the clock, he saw it was time to close up. He wished it were Saturday so he could head for Steve's for dinner with his brother and niece. Unfortunately, it was only Thursday. He decided to get a pizza on his way home.

The pizzeria was a low, grimy building with a few plastic booths, pool tables in the back, and the football game playing in the background. Pretty much a bar, but with pizza and calzones instead of hot wings.

Grayson gave his order to the bored-looking girl behind the counter, who seemed far too young to be working at this kind of joint.

"That'll be, like, five minutes." Her eyes dropped back to her phone.

Grayson shifted from one foot to the other. There was a group of guys behind him at one of the booths drinking beer and eating pizza, talking loudly about the football game that was on. They were young—seemed too young to be drinking to Grayson's eyes.

Two of them caught him looking, and Grayson shifted his own gaze away, fighting the urge to hunch protectively into his coat. Warning bells were going off in his head, telling him to make himself small, to get out of there as fast as he could. He became very aware of the fact that they were bigger than he was, younger, in better shape. And he was alone.

Did he pass from behind with his coat on? He didn't know. When they looked at him, did they see a man, a woman? The hot edge of panic crept up on him. He tried, tried so hard, but he didn't pass, and he knew it. He worked at being fine with that, telling himself there were more important things than passing as cisgender. And there were, but right now ... God, he hated this, everything about this and the way it made him feel.

"Here." The girl pushed a pizza box and white paper bag across the counter.

"Thanks." He pulled out his wallet and pushed a couple worn bills across the counter. "Keep the change."

She nodded, slightly more friendly, and Grayson grabbed his pizza.

The guys were still watching him, eating their pizza, attention no longer on the game.

Grayson carefully didn't look at them, didn't so much as glance in their direction as he pushed the door open with his shoulder and walked toward his car. He hated that he expected to hear footsteps come after him, hated the tightness in his shoulders, the way his body poised to spin and fight.

He closed his eyes, took a breath, and forced himself to walk slow and unhurried to his car.

No one came after him.

Still, it wasn't until he'd pulled out onto the main road, pizza stowed on the passenger seat beside him, that he finally breathed a sigh of relief.

On Mondays, Tuesdays, Wednesdays, Fridays, and as many weekends as he could work, Grayson got up, made himself a cup of coffee, and changed into dark work pants, black work boots, and a long-sleeved T-shirt.

The sky was gray that Friday, heavy with snow, the sun just a lighter strip of gray on the horizon. The birds had gone, the air quiet and waiting.

They were supposed to get snow in the afternoon, so Grayson pulled on his heavy woolen coat.

Schroder's supermarket sat in a tiny plaza along with a Laundromat, a bar, and a Chinese restaurant. It was locally owned and small, with only three checkout lines. Not even the locals shopped exclusively there. They drove into Binghamton to go to the Wegmans. But it was a good place to swing by if you forgot milk and were running late.

In the back room, Grayson pulled on his hairnet and white butcher's jacket.

Darleen was already behind the deli counter bent over a bowl, her small, bony arms mixing a huge mound of egg salad with surprising vigor. Just about the only thing that Schroder's was known for was the deli salads. People would crowd into the store come lunchtime. There would be hunters dressed head to toe in camo, often with their sons, sometimes as young as six. They'd buy lunch, along with bottles of the sour, vinegar-heavy sauce this part of New York preferred, ready to marinate the venison they hoped to get later that day. There would be local cops and little old ladies, truck drivers from off the highway, people sent over from the factory just down the road to pick up lunch.

Everyone had told Grayson when he started working here how lucky he was to be learning the secret recipes for Schroder's potato salad, macaroni salad, coleslaw, and egg salad.

He didn't feel lucky.

"Go grab the macaroni out of the refrigerator." Darleen frowned at him. But then, in the five years Grayson had worked here, he hadn't ever seen her smile.

"Yeah, I can do the macaroni salad if you want to do the potato and egg salads." Grayson pulled on a pair of plastic gloves on his way into the back of the store.

"All right, but I have to taste it before it goes into the case," Darleen called back to him. "If it's not perfect, I'll be the one in trouble, you know?"

Of course, Grayson thought, hauling the huge bowls of cooked pasta out of the fridge. This wasn't his first day of work, even if Darleen always acted like it was.

Robert pushed the back door open, wrestling on his hairnet.

"Hey." Grayson glanced up at him briefly. "You want to make sure all the cheese and meat is sliced?"

"Yeah." Robert stepped into the front of the deli, so tall he had to duck through the doorway.

Grayson slopped mayonnaise into the bowl of pasta, cut eggs, added some sweet pickle juice, plenty of salt and pepper, and celery salt.

"Grace!" Darleen bellowed. "Grace, get out here and help Robert with the deli slices!"

He froze at the sound of his legal name. People used it here because he'd been afraid five years ago that they wouldn't give him a job if they knew he was trans. He'd been pre-everything then, and it had hurt, but it had also made sense.

Now it was like being slapped in the face.

"I'm coming." He wrestled plastic wrap over the top of the bowl.

He stopped just before stepping into the front of the deli to take several deep breaths.

It's just a name, he told himself. *It doesn't mean anything, and it's better if they don't know because you need this job.*

Darleen and Robert waited by the slicer.

"There she is." Darleen turned toward him. "Show Robert how to slice cheese the correct way again. He keeps doing it wrong."

"Here." Grayson had to stand on his toes to reach the handle of the slicer. "Like this." He demonstrated for Robert. "See how I'm doing it? Not too much pressure, but just enough. Here, you try."

Robert did a few slices, and Grayson inspected them. "That's really good, just keep doing it like that and you'll be fine." He patted Robert on the back.

"Thanks."

"Is that macaroni salad done yet?" Darleen asked.

"Not yet."

Darleen shook her head with a disapproving frown.

Grayson went to the back to finish the macaroni salad.

Grayson could hear the happy yelling as soon as he turned into Steve's driveway the following afternoon.

When he pushed open the front door, Emily and Lisa threw themselves at him, screaming.

"Uncle Grayson!" they both shrieked at the top of their lungs.

"Hi, you two." He bent to hug them back.

"Hey." Steve stood in the doorway to the kitchen, smiling at him from behind his beard.

"Thanks for having me over." Grayson untangled himself from Emily and Lisa.

"Sure. Anytime. Want a beer?"

"Yeah." Grayson followed his brother into the kitchen. "Where's Rebecca?"

Steve gave a half shrug. "Having an evening with her friend. I told her we could watch the kids."

Grayson suspected she wasn't here because he was. Rebecca came from a very conservative Christian family and had taken his coming out and transition only slightly better than Grayson's parents.

One day, she's going to put her foot down. Grayson's fingers curled around the cool bottle of beer Steve handed him.

Lisa hollered from the other room, and for a moment Grayson was terrified this might be the last time he ever saw them. He shook his head, dispelling his fears, at least for the time being.

"So how's work?" Steve bent over to pull the meat-loaf from the oven.

"It's fine." Grayson took a sip of his beer.

"You're doing some commission work, right?"

"I was, but ..." He rubbed the hand not holding his beer across his jaw. "I don't know. I couldn't find what they were looking for and ... it's personal."

"Personal?" Steve's full attention was on him now, a small frown between his eyes.

Not trying-to-kill-myself personal, Grayson wanted to snap. He hated that Steve looked at him that way, hated that he'd given Steve a reason to. At the end of the day, Steve was just looking out for him like he always had. Steve had taken care of him after he'd gotten out of the hospital. Steve had given him a home, helped him find a job, allowed him to live in the trailer and not pay rent. Steve had always been there when their parents hadn't, when their sister hadn't. Because that was, after all, what big brothers did for little brothers.

"I went on a date."

Some of the worry cleared from Steve's face. "Good, that's good. Isn't it?"

"It didn't go well." Grayson wanted to shut his eyes against the memory of the look on Wyatt's face, but even more than that he didn't want to remember Wyatt's long hands, the way he bent to listen to

Grayson as he talked, the darkness of his eyes, the curve of his mouth ...

"Oh." Steve's face fell. "I'm sorry, but you know there are plenty of other opportunities." He clapped Grayson on the shoulder.

Grayson didn't have the heart to point out that people weren't exactly falling over themselves to date trans historians with no social life.

Steve was sweet, kind, and tall, with the sort of muscular physique everyone loved. Most of all, though, he was straight, and even before Rebecca, Grayson couldn't remember a time when Steve hadn't had a girlfriend.

Lisa and Emily rushed yelling into the room and attached themselves to Grayson. "Come play!" they chorused.

"You okay with dinner?"

"I'll be fine." Steve waved them off, already getting out the cutting board. Grayson let Lisa and Emily pull him from the kitchen.

"What do you want to play?" he asked.

"House!" Emily shrieked.

"Okay." Grayson followed them into the playroom, where they had a little kitchen set and a baby cradle in the corner.

"Lisa can be the baby." Two years older, Emily ignored the way Lisa glared at her. "And I can be the big girl." She turned to Grayson. "And you can be the daddy."

Lisa turned to Emily. "But who will be the mommy?"

"Maybe there isn't a mommy," he said. Both girls stared at him like he'd sprouted a second head. "Or maybe there are two daddies."

"No." Emily crossed her little arms over her chest. "I have a mommy and a daddy, Lisa has a mommy and a daddy, all my friends have mommies and daddies. There's only mommies and daddies."

Grayson was caught aback by how forcefully she said it, as if he were somehow trying to trick her into believing something that wasn't true.

But then again, why would she believe him? For the part of her life she could remember, he'd been single, and he'd mostly dated people of the opposite sex anyway. If she saw him now with his last girl-friend, she would see a boy and a girl together just like her mom and dad. All her books portrayed het-erosexual couples taking care of children, as did her TV shows. He was sure she knew kids from single-parent households, but were there any children from same-sex households at her school, among her friends? He doubted it. She went to a tiny rural school.

"Some families do have two daddies," he said cau-tiously. Her frown only grew.

"No." Her tone made it clear she was laying down the law. "There isn't."

"And some families have two mommies." It was a last-ditch hope. Emily was shaking her head as soon as the words came out of his mouth.

"You can be the daddy"—she pointed at him—"and I'll be the mommy, and Lisa can be the baby."

"You sure you want me to be the daddy and you to be the mommy and not you be the daddy?" Grayson asked more as a joke than anything else and was taken aback again when Emily became angry enough to stamp her foot.

"No, you're the boy, you need to be the daddy. I'm a girl, so I'm the mommy."

"Oh, honey." He didn't even know where to begin. It felt good that he was very definitely a man in her eyes. On the other hand ...

He reached out and hugged her. "You can be a daddy if you want."

"No, you be the daddy." She pulled away and handed him a dish. "Now wash the dishes."

He crawled to the little plastic sink and pretended to wash the plastic dishes.

"Hey." Steve knocked on the doorframe. "You guys ready for dinner?"

"Yeah!" Emily and Lisa leapt up and ran to him.

"Go wash your hands." They stampeded to the bathroom.

Grayson stood more slowly, his joints popping.

"You okay down there?" Steve was grinning at him.

"Feeling like I'm too old to be sitting on the floor."

Steve held out his hand to help Grayson all the way up.

"Meatloaf!" The girls charged back into the room. Steve laughed and let them pull him into the kitchen.

Steve had set the kitchen table. There were even real cloth napkins, if mismatched. The meatloaf sat on the table along with mashed potatoes and salad.

"Nice. Even salad." Grayson sat, and Steve helped Lisa into her highchair and Emily into her booster seat.

"It just came out of a bag, nothing fancy." He scooped some potatoes onto Lisa's plate and set it aside to cool. "Who else wants potatoes?"

Emily and Grayson raised their hands. Steve dished potatoes while Grayson reached for the salad tongs.

"Emily, you want salad?" He offered some to her, but she shook her head.

"I don't like it."

"Have a little salad." Steve helped Lisa cut up her meatloaf.

"I don't like it." Emily kicked her feet and shoveled potatoes into her mouth with her hand.

Grayson and Steve exchanged a glance. "Okay." Steve put a forkful of meatloaf into his mouth. "If you change your mind, let me know."

The landline phone rang, and Steve stood to pick it up.

"Hello?" He glanced at the three of them still at the table. "Oh, hey, Mary." Cradling the phone against his ear, he stepped into the next room.

Grayson's body had gone rigid, the hand not holding a fork clenched into a fist. He was being stupid. Of course Steve still talked to her. She was their sister. Steve didn't try to hide the relationship he still had with their family, even though Grayson ... didn't.

Minutes passed as Grayson watched Emily finish off her mashed potatoes and start on handfuls of meatloaf. Lisa smeared her food around on the tray of her highchair without eating much of it. Grayson didn't even try to touch his food. His stomach had cramped itself into knots too badly for him to get anything down.

After what felt like a lifetime, Steve stuck his head back into the kitchen. He looked unhappy and a little bit confused. "She wants to talk to you."

"Who? Me?" Grayson put his hand on his chest.

Steve nodded. "Yeah, but I told her if you didn't want to talk to her, she can't push it. You've got a better reason than she does not to want to talk to her."

Grayson glanced at the kids, who'd stopped eating and were definitely listening now. Then he followed Steve into the other room.

"Do you want me to hang up?" Steve asked. "Or tell her no? Because I can do either."

"No." Grayson reached for the phone, although he had no idea what he was going to say. "I'll talk to her."

Steve looked like he wanted to argue but handed the phone to Grayson anyway. It was cool against his face, larger than the cell phones he was used to. "Hello."

"Grace?" Mary sounded stiff, almost formal, and just like that, Grayson knew how the rest of the conversation was going to go. "How are you? Rebecca mentioned you were coming over to visit the kids today."

Next to him, Steve crossed his arms, mouth set in an angry frown.

"Yeah." Grayson rubbed one hand across his forehead. "We're having dinner."

There was a long pause.

"Mom's been asking about you." Mary was trying to be civil, but the fact that he could hear the strain of it in her voice made him want to hang up, or cry, or possibly throw up. Instead, he closed his eyes and tightened his grip on the phone.

"Really?"

Mary sniffed. "We've been planning Thanksgiving. She wishes we could all be together, like a family. It's been a very long time since we were all together for Thanksgiving."

Grayson forced himself to breathe evenly, in and out, in and out. "Well." *She was the one who told me I was sick, that I was broken, that I couldn't be part of the family if I was going to do this to myself. And by 'this' she meant transition—be who I am.*

"I'd be willing to come for Thanksgiving." Grayson tried to sound calm. "But you know perfectly well if I come, no 'Grace.' It's Grayson. No 'she,' no expecting me to wear a dress or dress in women's clothes, and under no circumstances will I go to church with you all."

"Be reasonable," Mary hissed. "Mother is trying to be nice, mend fences, reach out to you. Don't throw it back in her face."

So this was the new deal, then. After a few years of ignoring his existence, his parents were ready to take him back into the family as long as everyone could pretend like nothing had happened and ignore his identity completely. He backed up a step to lean against the wall and closed his eyes.

"Look." Mary had obviously wrestled her temper back under control. "We're not asking you to change, we're asking you to just not rub it in anyone's face for one day. Less than that. You could just show up for dinner and let Mom and Dad have that."

It was so tempting. He wanted Christmas and Thanksgiving again, the way it had been when he was a kid. The house warm with the smell of food, loud with people talking and not fighting for once. He'd had the day off from school and later a break from college. It had been so nice to sink into that, help Mary peel potatoes and drink cheap wine while their mother fussed over the turkey.

But agreeing to this wouldn't bring that back.

"Mom and Dad can have me over at Thanksgiving or Christmas or whenever they want." Grayson wasn't even angry, although he could feel the anger radiating off Steve beside him. He was just resigned. "But this is my identity, and it's non-negotiable. You all either accept it or you don't."

There was a long silence on the other end of the phone.

"Well," Mary said finally. "Seems like you've already made up your mind about not wanting to be part of this family anymore."

The line went dead.

"What did she say?" Steve asked.

"Mom and Dad want me over for Thanksgiving." Grayson stared down at the phone in his hand. "But … they want to pretend like nothing happened and I couldn't, you know I can't."

"Yeah." Steve's hand met his shoulder. "I know. If that's what they wanted, you, uh, you did the right thing telling them no."

Grayson didn't know if he had or not. He just rubbed his face, not sure if he wanted to cry, punch something, or get a drink.

Steve went back into the kitchen. Grayson could hear him talking to the girls. When he came out, he had two mashed-potato-covered children in tow.

"Gotta clean the girls up." He sounded apologetic. Grayson just nodded.

"I'll start on the dishes."

"You don't have to."

"I want to."

It was soothing, at least: the ritual of running dishes under the water and wiping them with a soapy sponge.

Steve came back while Grayson was scrubbing out the meatloaf pan.

"Where are the girls?"

"In the living room, watching TV." Steve picked up a dishcloth and started drying. "Hey, there's something I've been meaning to talk to you about. Should have done it before, actually. Now ..." Steve winced.

"What?" Grayson handed the pot over and started on the silverware.

"It's about Thanksgiving." Steve hesitated. "I know we spent it together last year, but this year Mom and

Dad want us to bring the girls over to theirs. I was going to tell you, and then I guess it all went to shit when Mary called. But I thought you should know."

Grayson had frozen for a moment. Now he continued to wash, rubbing the soapy sponge up and down each fork before rinsing it under the water. "Okay."

"Is it okay?" Steve put down the cloth and rested one hip against the counter. "I could tell them no. I mean, I'm half thinking of telling them no anyway after that stunt Mary pulled—"

"It's all right. I'll be fine." Grayson rinsed off the last of the forks and put them in the drainer. "And you should go. They're your family."

"They're your family, too." Steve seemed to vibrate with anger. "Or at least they should be."

Grayson didn't answer.

Steve sighed. "You blame yourself."

It wasn't a question, and the fact that Grayson didn't correct him only seemed to make Steve angrier. "You fucking shouldn't, because it's not your fault. You were in the fucking hospital, and they still blamed you. They're your family. They're supposed to take care of you."

Grayson was glad the girls were in the living room, because Steve's voice was getting louder with every word.

"I tried to kill myself." He was so tired of all of this. "I didn't have cancer."

"Shouldn't matter." Steve slammed the utensil drawer hard enough for it to rattle. "You were sick and you needed help, and all they could talk about was how this was going to affect their lives and what the people at their church were going to say. I'm not pretending like I have the whole trans thing figured out yet, but it took me like fifteen minutes on the computer to know I just needed to ask you about the pronouns and name stuff and go with whatever you said. But that's fifteen minutes more than Mary's willing to spend, and she's your goddamn sister."

Grayson sat at the table and put his face in his hands. Behind him, Steve sucked in a long breath and then released it in a sigh. "I'm sorry. It just makes me angry."

"Yeah." Grayson didn't lift his head, but he did turn to look at Steve. "It makes me angry, too."

Steve sat next to him and gave his shoulder an awkward squeeze. "Do you have anyone else you could spend Thanksgiving with? Friends … ?" He trailed off. Grayson studied the old Formica of the tabletop for a moment.

"Don't worry about it." He stood and touched Steve's shoulder on the way by. "Go, have the girls celebrate with their grandparents. Don't worry about me."

He headed for the living room to see what Emily and Lisa were up to.

They were cuddled on the couch watching *Thomas the Tank Engine*. He sat between them and watched, too. Lisa curled up against him, dozing off. Emily also began to look sleepy.

"I need to go soon." He leaned over and gave Emily a little one-armed hug, trying not to wake Lisa. Emily made a small sound of protest. Grayson gave her another hug. Moving Lisa carefully, he detangled himself from them.

Steve met him at the front door. "Thanks for coming."

"No, thanks for having me." Grayson pulled on his boots and coat. "It was fun."

"Yeah." Steve looked like he wanted to say something else, but just clapped Grayson on the shoulder again.

"Daddy?" Emily called from the living room. Lisa started crying.

Grayson gave Steve a little wave and pulled the front door closed behind him.

"Hey, you."

Grayson was filling up the display bowl with more potato salad.

"Hey, you."

He turned to see a group of men by the deli counter. They were maybe eighteen or nineteen, four of them dressed in hunting gear.

"What would you gentlemen like?"

The one in front of the group smirked at him in a way that made his skin crawl. "A pound of macaroni salad and a pound of potato."

Grayson just nodded and scooped the salads into containers. He weighed them and punched in the numbers so the labels would print out.

"Hey."

He looked up, startled. The young man who'd put in the order was at the counter again. "Hey, you have a boyfriend?"

Don't back up, Grayson told himself, stiffening his spine. "No." He gave the young man his most unfriendly scowl.

The predatory grin was back. Up close, Grayson could see that the guy was growing that downy, patchy stubble sported by boys newly capable of facial hair. He reevaluated his estimation of their age.

"I would make a good boyfriend," the boy said. "Maybe I could be yours?" It wasn't even really a question.

Grayson's skin crawled, the misgendering mixed with harassment causing his stomach to lurch and knot.

He looked the dude up and down slowly and then let his lip curl. "I don't think so," he said, and slammed their containers onto the top of the counter.

The friends laughed. The young man's smirk dropped to become uglier. He said something low and vicious under his breath and lunged, reaching for Grayson, who backed up so fast he almost fell.

"What is going on here?" Both Grayson and the cluster of young men jumped. Grayson looked around to see Darleen bearing down on them from the back room of the store.

"He said—" Grayson started, and Darleen cut him off.

"I heard what he said." She glared daggers at the young men, who were looking at the ground now. "Will that be all?"

They muttered something, grabbed the containers, and shuffled off.

Darleen turned back to Grayson. "Are you all right?"

"Excuse me." Grayson fled into the back, toward the employee bathrooms. There was a handicapped bathroom, a single-room toilet nobody used. Grayson locked himself in and backed up until he was sitting on the toilet.

"Fuck!" His hands were shaking, his whole body was shaking, and he put his hands up to cover his face, hoping he wasn't going to have a panic attack.

"Fuck! Fuck!" He doubled over, rocking himself back and forth, until his breathing finally calmed.

There was a knock on the door, and Grayson forced himself to stand. Forced himself to unlock the door.

Darleen stood on the other side. "Are you all right? Did that young man touch you?"

"He didn't." Grayson smoothed the front of his work clothes. "I'm okay."

"Good." She made a move like she was going to pat him, then dropped her arm to the side. "Good," she said again. "I have some work on the salads for tomorrow for you today, okay? You can stay in the back until your shift's over if you want. I'll handle the customers."

"Thanks." He felt like a little bit of a coward hiding in the back, but he was also still jittery with nerves.

"Okay." Darleen gave him one last look, nodded curtly, and straightened her hairnet over her gray hair before she pushed the kitchen door open.

Grayson took a long breath and then stepped into the kitchen.

CHAPTER 7

On Thursday, Grayson turned on his computer at the historical society to find an email from Rachel. She'd sent him links and a list of books to look for.

For a long time, he just stared at the email. He didn't have to do this anymore. Wyatt was ... gone, so he wasn't waiting for any of this research.

He wrote up a short email thanking Rachel, then closed out the program. There was cataloging he needed to do. He might as well get to that.

Hours later, he'd made some headway, but mostly he'd just done busywork, his mind all over the place. Finally, with only a few minutes left of the day, his whole body almost vibrating and light with contained energy, he got up and started wandering through the stacks, letting his fingers smooth over objects and books.

One of the reasons he'd taken the job here was to stay close to the profession, but also because the collection was such a cluttered and disorganized mess. No one had been in here doing anything other than just stacking donated things on the nearest clear surface for years. Grayson had wanted the challenge of it: the act of taking chaos and reworking it into something beautiful and good was what history was all about. He needed to remember that, hold it close and let it live inside him again. Hadn't he fallen in love with history because it wasn't simple or easy?

Over time, he'd let the details overwhelm him. He'd gotten to the point where filling out spreadsheets was more important than the research. Where the finer points inside the chaos blinded him to the bigger picture, disguising its beauty.

What had he been doing for the last few years? What was he doing now?

He shut down his computer and gathered up his stuff.

It had snowed in the night, and there was ice and snow on the ground. Dusk turned the sky the same color as the snow-covered ground. The trees along the road were silhouetted in black against the gray sky.

The house was dark and cold when he got there, and Grayson wandered through the tiny space flipping on lights and turning on the heat. The pool of warm yellow light from the lamps in the living room and by his desk spilled out the front windows, tinting the ice and snow on the ground with gold warmth.

He wished he had good crockpot stew recipe. How nice would it be to come home to the house filled up with the smell of cooking stew? Instead, he dug out a can of tomato soup and poured it into a pot before fixing himself a cheese sandwich to grill. The kitchen heated as the stove did.

When his soup was hot, he took his meal into the living room space and curled up in his armchair. He turned on his computer, balancing the bowl of soup on his knees.

Outside, the wind blew the branches of the trees around his house together. They clacked like bones, scraping along his tin roof. Grayson felt too hot, his skin creeping with a prickle of anxiety. The wind knocked on the windows, and Grayson controlled his breathing until a little bit of calmness settled in his chest.

What they said about trans people knowing from the time they were children wasn't always true. When he thought back on it, he'd always known something was wrong—always had an unease that rose up inside him when someone called him a girl—but he hadn't had words for it.

Back then, he'd only been focused on work, the opportunity to leave here, to go to a good college—a private college. That was the dream, even though only his mother had ever been to college, and she'd dropped out after a year and a half when she'd become pregnant with Steve.

Grayson had done it, too: gone to a nice private college, discovered history and research, and after that it had been easy to apply to graduate school. The plan had become a career in academia.

But now here he was. No PhD, no job in academia, back in the same town he'd grown up in, making so little money that Steve looked well-off by comparison.

He'd screwed up. But no—that wasn't quite it, because it hadn't been something he'd done—the crawling, sinking feeling that had only gotten more and more unbearable as time went on. The feeling that something was wrong, something wasn't right, not right the way he moved through the world, the way people looked at him, not quite right about his own skin. The sense of wrongness, of not fitting, not being—he wasn't anything when his girlfriend put her arms around him and snuggled close, whispered what a beautiful woman he wasn't. He didn't exist, no names, no words, no space. This world wasn't built with space in it for what he was, not even cracks left to live in, to see himself. It crushed in on him, the unhappiness, the inability to make himself care, to make himself move, the creeping dark that came from knowing you didn't exist in this world. It had eaten his time and stolen from him the life he'd been so excited to live.

I've lost my place, Grayson thought, panic rising suddenly ice cold in his chest. *I've lost my place and I don't know, I don't know.*

He put his hands over his eyes and pressed until light exploded at the edges of the dark, white ringed in tarnished yellow.

Next to him, his phone buzzed, the sound cutting through his thoughts and jolting him back to his warm living room, soup and sandwich slowly going cold in his lap. Grayson juggled the bowl and plate down onto the ground, then reached for his phone.

WYATT KELLY

He froze, and then for a wild moment wanted to just let it ring. His finger was pressing the answer button, though, before he'd worked out what it was he really wanted to do.

He cleared his throat and held the phone up to his ear. "Hello?"

"Hey."

He could definitely hear the nervous energy in Wyatt's voice.

"I know you probably don't want to hear from me, but I need you to listen for a minute, okay? I want to apologize. I know I was a dick, but I got scared and panicked a little bit. I do that sometimes when I get scared—I panic." It all came out in a long rush. "Anyway, I wanted to call and apologize and say it's not you, there is nothing wrong with you, I mean, I really like you."

"Uh," was the only thing Grayson could think of to say.

The noise on the other end behind Wyatt went indistinct, and he could hear Wyatt say, "okay, okay," but soft, like he'd pulled the phone away from his face, and then the whoosh of Wyatt sighing.

"The thing is." Wyatt must have put the phone back, because Grayson could hear him better now. "I'm trans, too, but I'm kind of deep in the closet, and I've never dated anyone who knew before. But I wanted you to know, and it ... it got inside my head. I don't know, it sounds stupid now."

Grayson leaned forward so he could cradle his face in his free hand. "It's okay. I get it."

"Yeah?" On the other end, Wyatt sounded unbearably hopeful and far too young.

"Coming out is hard." Hard, and painful, and so much of the time Grayson wondered why he'd done it at all, especially when it came to his parents. "I've never had a partner who knew either."

They were both silent for a moment, Grayson thinking about what that admission might mean.

There was freedom in admitting that this was new territory for both of them. Relief, too, that there was someone else who understood.

"I just didn't want you to think I didn't like you," Wyatt said, soft and sweet.

That made Grayson smile, his body lightening a little. "It's all good."

"I'd love to try again." Wyatt still sounded so hopeful. "If you'd be willing to maybe start again from the beginning?"

Grayson was grinning now, so wide it almost hurt. "Yeah, I'd like that."

"Let's start over. I'm Wyatt. I'm a nonbinary, feminine trans person."

"Hi." It was ridiculous, but still shyness and a little bit of nerves tightened his throat as he spoke. He wished he could see Wyatt. "I'm just a regular old trans dude, I guess."

"I, uh, I've never asked anyone this, but …" Nervousness had crept back into Wyatt's voice. "Could you use 'they' and 'them' pronouns? For me?"

Grayson's smile gentled. "Of course."

On the other end of the phone, Wyatt sighed, like letting go of a breath they'd been holding for a very long time.

Hi, Wyatt. It's me. I've been doing some thinking about your photograph, and I think I'm going to go up to Lily Dale within the next couple weeks to talk to some of the historians up there. I would love it if you wanted to come, if you can take the time, uh, yeah.

Wyatt stared at their phone for a few long seconds, not sure they'd heard correctly. They'd already played the message back a few times just to make sure Grayson was really inviting them to go to Lily Dale, of all places, with him. Plus, there was the part when Grayson's voice trailed off for a split second, then speeded up to pretty much as fast as a human could talk, bouncing and stuttering over the word "love." Wyatt had to listen to it twice just to be sure "love" was in fact what Grayson had said.

Could they go to Lily Dale? Google said it was a three-hour drive one way. Would the two of them have to stay overnight? Wyatt had been going around to their mother's apartment on the weekend mornings to make sure she was all right and taking her medication. If they weren't going to be there on a weekend morning, they'd have to get Jess to do it instead. But deep down, they'd wanted to go up and see Lily Dale since Grayson had told them about it.

And seeing Grayson again ... Wyatt's stomach turned over, not unpleasantly, but there were some nerves there, too. They'd made a fool of themselves on their date with Grayson, not to mention being a dick. On the other hand ... the two of them had made up, hadn't they? Grayson had been so gracious, more gracious than he could have known, and reached out right when Wyatt needed him to. Wyatt had been embraced in the moment when they most needed that comfort and connection—not as an empty gesture but a fullness that said, *I understand*. Until that moment, Wyatt hadn't admitted, not even to themselves, what they needed. Hearing Grayson speak of them the way they truly were was like being held for the first time.

Wyatt sighed, putting the phone on the coffee table, and let themselves slowly slide sideways until they were lying on the couch. It was late. They should get up and make themselves dinner, change out of their work clothes, but right now they didn't really feel like moving. They laced their fingers together on their stomach and stared up at the ceiling. If they got up, they'd be able to locate a bottle of wine, but on the other hand they were comfortable where they were. Their gaze went to their phone. They should call Grayson back. Was it too late tonight? But they had work tomorrow, and Judge Mayer didn't love them making personal calls. They stuck out one arm and swiped the phone off the coffee table without bothering to sit up.

They pressed CALL on Grayson's number before they could talk themselves out of it. It rang on

Grayson's side three times before there was a click and Grayson's voice on the line. "Hello, Wyatt?" He sounded a little bit tentative and unsure.

Wyatt put their phone on speaker and laid it on their chest. "Hey, how are you?"

"I'm okay. Good, actually." Grayson sounded tired. He'd looked tired the times they'd met in person, too—tired, serious, maybe a little bit angry and a little bit sad. He didn't sound angry or sad today. Possibly, he even sounded happy.

Wyatt hoped at least a little of that happiness came from talking to them.

"I got your message about Lily Dale, and I would love to go with you."

"Oh." Grayson sounded surprised. "Okay, great, we should, uh ... what date would work for you?"

"Next weekend?" It was probably the soonest they'd be able to get stuff settled. "Yeah, that should work."

"Next weekend will probably be all right," Grayson said. "Let me email the curator at the Lily Dale museum and see if Saturday works."

"Okay." Wyatt felt new at this, like it was somehow the first time the two of them had talked. But a fresh start had been what they'd wanted, hadn't it? "I'm really looking forward to it—really looking forward to seeing you." They cringed a little at how that sounded.

On the other end of the phone, Grayson laughed. "I'm excited about seeing you again, too."

"Yeah?" Relief washed over them.

"Of course," Grayson said, laughter still in his voice. "I can't wait. And thanks for calling me. I look forward to seeing you for our trip."

"Yeah." Wyatt gripped the phone tight.

"I, uh ... I look forward to it," Grayson said.

That eased the knot in their chest. "You said that already." Grayson huffed on the other end, and Wyatt couldn't help smiling. "It's all right, I'm looking forward to it, too."

Grayson made a sound between a snort and a laugh. "That was bad." But his voice was warm with humor. "But I'm okay with it."

Wyatt laughed, too. "I'm glad I have your approval."

"You do. I, uh, should let you get back to whatever you were doing."

"I guess I'll see you later, then." Wyatt was still smiling and felt like maybe they would never stop. "Have a good night."

"You, too." Grayson hesitated like he wanted something else, but then hung up.

Wyatt laid there for a few seconds longer before getting up and making their way to the kitchen. They poked around the freezer until they came up with a frozen curry. They filled their rice cooker with rice and water and turned it on, then poured themselves a glass of wine.

One of these days, they should take some time off. The last time they'd had a vacation, they'd spent it moving their mother into her apartment. But maybe next time they got time off they could do something fun with it, like bake bread, finish tiling the kitchen, or cook a meal from scratch just for them. Maybe they'd get to cook for Grayson, or at least bring him some bread. Wyatt thought they'd like that—making them both dinner sometime.

They needed to do a really in-depth clean of the whole apartment, actually. The bathroom was in dire need of a scrubbing, not the quick wipe down they tried to get to once a week. The living room could do with a thorough vacuuming as well. Maybe they should figure out when they would next be owed time and talk to Judge Mayer about it. They could even take a long weekend. A long weekend of cleaning and cooking sounded pathetically good at this point.

It had been so long since they'd taken time for themselves, let their life settle into something balanced and good. There was a lightness inside them now, though.

It felt like time to start figuring out how to do that.

Wyatt hadn't been sure what they'd been expecting when Grayson told them to drive up to Grayson's house so they could carpool to Lily Dale.

Grayson's house was off a narrow, nearly dirt road that ran between fields, glittering with frost in the early morning light. It was nestled in a small grove of trees, and when Wyatt pulled up in front they realized how small it was. It wasn't really a house but a trailer, with white plastic siding beginning to go brown where dirt and rust had stained it. Wyatt sat in their car for a moment, just looking, as any idea that Grayson came from money fled. Then they pulled the keys free of the ignition and pushed the car door open.

As soon as Wyatt got out of the car, Grayson opened his door. "You want to come in?"

Wyatt did want to see what the inside of the house looked like, even though Grayson's tone was wary. "Sure."

So Grayson stepped back, letting them in.

There was a mat right in front of the door to catch tracked-in mud and snow. Wyatt bent to take off their boots. When they straightened back up, they got a good look at the inside of the house.

It was as small as they'd thought it was. There was a window next to the door and another across from it. The rest of the living room wall space was solid bookcases. A battered couch sat on one side of the room with some kind of long, old-fashioned trunk being used as a coffee table. Through the doorway to the right, Wyatt could see what looked to be a small, window-filled kitchen.

"It's not much." Wyatt could see Grayson's nervousness in the way he held himself. "But you know, I'm lucky to have it. My brother technically owns it, but he rents it to me."

"It's nice." Wyatt rubbed their hands together, trying to fight off the early morning chill that had numbed their fingers.

"Thank you." Grayson actually blushed, turning his face away. "Want some tea or coffee before we get going?"

"Do you have coffee?" They'd left their apartment with only one cup in their system instead of their daily three. "Don't worry about making fresh if you don't, though."

"I do have some." Grayson moved to the kitchen and took a coffee cup off a hook on the wall. "Sugar? Half and half?"

"Both, please." Wyatt perched on one of the chairs. A table folded down from the wall to their left. "A spoonful of sugar, splash of cream. Or, you know, I can do it."

"It's fine." Grayson splashed in the half and half, added the sugar, and brought the cup over.

"The historian I spoke with said she'd meet us at one." Grayson sat on the chair next to Wyatt. "It's going to be nearly three hours' drive for us, so we should leave soon."

"Yeah." Wyatt glanced up at the clock, then tried to gulp down the coffee as fast as they could without burning the roof off their mouth. The coffee burned as it went down their throat anyway.

They started coughing, and Grayson reached out to grasp their shoulder. "You okay?"

Wyatt gasped and fought back the tears. Grayson had moved to stand beside them, really quite close. He was wearing a blue button-up shirt and a midnight blue vest that looked like silk. There were little flowers embroidered in a thread just a bit lighter than the silk all around the edge of the waistcoat. Bent over, Wyatt was at eye level with a silver pin shaped like some kind of winged insect right where the breast pocket would be. It moved as Grayson breathed.

It made them feel slightly self-conscious about their own appearance, though they'd dressed carefully this morning. They wore skinny jeans, a cream button-up with a green stripe just wider than a pinstripe, an oatmeal V-neck sweater, and a skinny tie in the same green as the stripe. It wasn't what they'd wear if they were staying in, but it made them look pretty, they thought.

Grayson's hand was warm and comforting on their shoulder. The feel of it distracted Wyatt from worrying about their clothes.

They straightened, feeling a little bit red. "We should get going."

"Okay." Grayson dropped his hand from Wyatt's shoulder. "You want to bring your coffee with you?"

Wyatt felt his flush deepen. "Sure, if you don't mind."

Grayson only shrugged.

He had the directions up on his phone and Wyatt's cup of coffee in one hand as Wyatt guided their car back onto the road.

Lily Dale was in the westernmost part of the state, about an hour south of Buffalo.

"So are you and your brother close?" Wyatt asked when they hit the highway.

"Yes." Grayson nodded. "We are. He's been very supportive of me and my transition. I'm really close with my nieces, too. I go over to their house fairly often, actually."

They lapsed into silence.

"And you have a sister?" Grayson asked.

"Yes, Jess. She's a few years older than me, but we're pretty close." Wyatt looked across to Grayson. "You want to put on the radio?"

Grayson put the coffee into the cup holder and flipped the radio on. The first station was Christian rock coming in scratchy. After that, he flipped past three country stations.

"One thing I've never understood"—Grayson flipped to a classic rock station—"is why there's so many country music stations in Upstate New York. I mean, it's hard to be any more northern than we are without actually ending up in Canada."

They thought about that while the Rolling Stones played in the background.

"It could be because country music speaks to a working-class culture," Grayson offered as an answer to his own question. He'd been looking out the window, but now he turned to Wyatt. Even though Wyatt didn't take their eyes off the road, they could feel Grayson studying them.

"Or country music is often about farming and rural life, and there are lots of farms and rural life in Upstate New York." They were driving by fields now, in fact, some filled with dried corn stalks ready to be cut, others with pumpkin and squash vines. There were mostly small family plots out here bordered by forest or creeks.

"Yeah, that, too," Grayson agreed and flipped to another station that was indeed country. They rode while the Civil Wars sang on the radio, coming across a little tinny in Wyatt's less-than-new car.

"What are you expecting to find in Lily Dale?" Wyatt finally asked.

"Probably nothing. But maybe if we're lucky we'll find more pictures or a mention of Liam somewhere. And even if we don't, it'll be a good way to find out more about New York spiritualism."

"A needle in a haystack." Wasn't that what Grayson had implied this kind of project was, back in the beginning? "Is that what historical research is always like?"

"Not always, but sometimes. I used to like that kind of research a lot."

"Used to? I think you still do."

Grayson was silent a moment. "Maybe."

Wyatt gathered their courage to ask a question they'd been wondering about since they'd met Grayson. "You have a master's in history, yeah?"

Grayson nodded.

"Have you ever thought about a PhD and, you know, teaching? Or was working at a historical society always the goal?"

For a long moment, Grayson was very still. "I was planning on getting a PhD." He looked down at his hands and then straight out at the road ahead of them. Anywhere but at Wyatt. "But I had a few months off after I graduated with my master's degree. I was supposed to apply to the PhD program, but instead I ended up coming out as trans, fighting with my family. My parents made it clear that I couldn't transition and live with them, but I was unemployed with no savings, and I—I got depressed, and it was bad, and it just got worse and worse." Grayson took a long, shaky breath. "Eventually I ended up living with Steve, and that was better, I could transition then, I got a job, Steve helped me find my house. Things ..." He trailed off as the silence spread between them.

"Oh, honey, I'm so sorry." Wyatt took one hand off the wheel and reached over for Grayson's. They gave Grayson what they hoped was a reassuring squeeze.

"Things are better now." Grayson sounded like he'd just realized it was true.

"I'm glad you're okay." It didn't seem like enough, but Grayson just nodded like it was and gave them a small smile.

"I am. I really am."

The countryside passed by, the gray strip of high-way cutting through pine forests and hills, running alongside train tracks and rivers. The country music played in the background.

Grayson was quiet, watching out the window. Wyatt still wasn't entirely sure what to say, but they wanted to take the unhappy stillness away from Grayson, make him smile, make him happy.

They changed highways, still heading west in a straight line across the state. Grayson fiddled with the radio, switching between Christian rock, country, and every once in a while a patchy classic rock station.

"I know we'll meet with the historian when we get there and poke around the museum, but afterward, you want to grab dinner?" Wyatt tried their best to keep their tone casual, like it was no big deal even, though their pulse stuttered with the possibility of a yes.

"I think that would be great." Grayson hesitated for a moment. "Like a date."

"Yes, like a date."

Grayson smiled, wide and bright, down at his hands. Wyatt smiled, too.

Lily Dale, it turned out, was picturesque. That was the only word Wyatt had for it. Everything was late Victorian or renovated to look like it, in bright candy colors, clean and ready for the tourists.

The museum was an equally quaint little schoolhouse, white, with two stories. It looked like in the summer it would have a flower garden out front, too, right by the sign. Wyatt parked in the small lot that ran along the side of the building.

A middle-aged woman, round, with red hair pulled up on top of her head, met them right inside the door.

"Susan." She held out her hand. "I hear you have some questions about spiritualism and early-twentieth-century mediums."

"Grayson Alexander." Grayson stepped forward and shook. "And yes, one medium in particular: Liam Devlin. He was one of the founding members of the Binghamton Spiritualist Society."

"Well, the name doesn't sound familiar"—Susan shook Wyatt's hand, too—"but I'll let you two take a look at our records and see if you can find anything."

Susan led the way through the museum. "The museum isn't usually open to the public this time of year, but we like to help out local historians. You can poke around, and then if you like we can go over to the assembly and you can see the documents and donations that aren't part of the exhibits."

They wandered through the small building looking at exhibits. There were some that were probably too general, like the women's suffrage exhibit. Some of them were actually about spiritualism and mediums, though. Wyatt bent over the cases, scrutinizing photographs.

Lots of black-and-white faces of serious-looking women in dresses with huge skirts and equally unsmiling men in suits and top hats. There were pictures of people sitting around tables in a parlor and standing together on the lawns outside buildings, no one looking like they were having a good time of it.

Ahead of him, Grayson had gone rigid. Wyatt hurried to see what he was looking at.

It was a collection of photographs exactly like all the other displays. Grayson was bent over the case, so close his breath fogged the glass and his nose almost brushed it. Then Wyatt saw.

It was a photograph of Liam, yellow and blurry, but recognizably him. Unlike the other two photographs they'd seen of him, this time he was in uniform. It looked like the ones Wyatt had seen in pictures of the Civil War except with a more Indiana Jones–type hat. He posed stiffly, as always, one arm on top of a small table.

"So he served in the army. That's a start. He's not wearing a dress sword, so not cavalry, but I don't know my uniforms well enough. I'm not even sure this is an army uniform and not navy." Grayson dug out his cell phone and turned to Susan. "Can I take a picture?"

"Sure."

He held up the phone and snapped some pictures. "I'm going to send these off to a friend of mine who knows his military history much better than I do." His fingers flew across the screen of his phone. "I'll also send him a picture of James when I get back."

Grayson had stepped away from the case to take the picture, his back brushing Wyatt's front, very close—close enough that they could smell the cologne Grayson wore. Tea and something darker, almost smoky underneath.

Wyatt took a breath, feeling the way it shuddered through them, the way the warmth from Grayson's body spread down their own.

Then Grayson moved to peer down at the photograph again, and Wyatt tried to collect themselves.

"How would knowing his military history help us? Liam and James met each other though the spiritualist group in Binghamton. They must have—that's the only thing that makes sense." Wyatt moved forward, too, leaning over Grayson's shoulder to look at the photograph. It brought them close again, and Wyatt wanted to lean even closer still, breathe him in. *Concentrate*, Wyatt told themselves. It wasn't the time.

"Knowing his military history can give us insight into a portion of his life, and it might also give us a lead on his background."

"Okay," Wyatt said, even though what they really wanted to know was what the relationship had been between Liam and James—not Liam's military background.

"It's probably another long shot." Grayson was frowning at his phone now. "The National Archives have some of this sort of thing, but if we'll be able to find him—who knows?"

The weight of what they were doing, the sheer amount of information they were going to have to sort through with no guarantee of finding anything, settled on Wyatt. Grayson had really meant it when he said sometimes there was nothing there to find.

But we've found three photographs, Wyatt told themselves. And they knew a little bit about James and a little bit about Liam. So maybe they weren't doing so bad after all.

"Would you like to see the stuff that hasn't made it to the museum?" Susan asked brightly.

"That would be great." Grayson put his phone away.

Susan led them up to the second floor. Much like at Grayson's historical society, there were boxes, folders, and filing cabinets full of stuff.

"What are we going to do?" Wyatt flipped through a three-ring binder that had photographs in clear protective sleeves.

"Start looking." Grayson pulled open a filing cabinet. "And keep looking until we've gone through as much as we can today or we find something."

"All of it?"

Grayson's lips quirked up in a smile, though he didn't turn to show it to Wyatt. "Yes, all of it. That's what you do when you do this sort of research."

"Is this the way all historical research is? Or are we just special?" Wyatt pulled a stack of three-ring binders off the top of one of the filing cabinets and started flipping through them.

"We're just special." Grayson closed one drawer of the filing cabinet and then squatted down to go through the other. "Lots of people do historical research about things on which there's already scholarship, so, like, secondary sources, or if they're doing new and original research it's on something with archived sources or a written source, like a letter or diary. The hardest kind of research is original research, where there's no known archive of related information, no secondary writing, and where you're basing your research on a nonwritten source, like a photograph."

"Have you ever done that kind of research before?"

Grayson snorted. "Of course not. Only a crazy person tries to do this. A master's student who actually wants to make anything out of their career wouldn't dare."

Wyatt thought about that while they flipped through binders of photographs. "So most queer history isn't like this."

"Some queer history isn't like this, for sure." Grayson started on another filing cabinet. "Gay people wrote letters and diaries too, some of which even talk about being gay. There's a lot of scholarship based on those sorts of sources, or newspaper articles, trial records, police reports."

That made sense, although Wyatt did wonder what 'a lot of research' meant when talking about queer history.

Grayson kept on talking. He slid into lecture mode easily. Not that they minded—it was almost always interesting and endearing.

"The issue, of course, is if you only use diaries, letters, memoirs, police reports, and so on, you're only ever getting a tiny, tiny percentage of the queer population, who are ninety-nine percent of the time white, cisgender men. Want to study anyone else, and yes, it will be like this." Grayson slammed a drawer closed. "It's basically luck, the people we know about or the fact they were arrested. But that's luck, too, when it comes down to it."

They searched in silence. Grayson finished with the filing cabinets and went to look through the boxes. Wyatt continued with the photographs. After about an hour, they'd seen more pictures of Lily Dale than they cared to think about, and many, many pictures of nineteenth-century mediums. The mediums turned out to be kind of disappointing. They were mostly conservatively dressed, dour white people, and not nearly as racy as Wyatt would have expected for a group of people said to have possessed supernatural powers.

Flipping a page, they found a portrait of a couple probably in their fifties, the man in a sober black suit, the woman in long skirts with a frilly little bonnet thing on her head. They were both frowning as if judging Wyatt for their very twenty-first-century thoughts.

Photography: the power to look like disapproving grandparents from beyond the grave.

Wyatt closed the binder and started on another.

By the time Susan came to get them, they were still far from having gone through everything.

Wyatt Googled restaurants on their phone while Grayson thanked Susan for showing them the museum and letting them look through their resources.

There was an Italian restaurant close to their motel. It looked like every other tiny Italian restaurant or pizzeria in Upstate New York, but the food got good reviews on Yelp.

"Let's stop off at the motel first and check in." Grayson buckled his seatbelt.

"Okay." Wyatt needed to call Jess anyway to make sure Mom was all right and had gotten her meds this morning.

The motel where they'd been able to find the cheapest rooms was generic, low gray buildings with rust red doors and a long, narrow parking lot in front of the rooms. A neon sign out by the road read ROOMS VACANT, a couple of bulbs missing, a few more stuttering on and off.

They climbed out of the car.

A lady in her fifties, her gray hair pulled back from her face, sat behind a divider of foggy glass in the little hut of an office.

She looked back and forth between them.

"We reserved a room." That's what they'd agreed, since it would be cheaper to split one room than to get two. Wyatt had anticipated it being awkward, but they didn't have the extra money lying around to say no when Grayson offered. It also made them feel better that Grayson had offered it at all.

"For how long?" The woman tapped a few keys on the ancient-looking computer in front of her.

"One night." Grayson sounded calm and professional, though he held himself a little too rigid. "It should be under Grayson Alexander. Do you need my credit card number?"

She looked between the two of them again. She must have sensed some queerness somewhere—whether it was them or Grayson, Wyatt couldn't tell—but either way, her eyes narrowed behind her glasses. "You said you wanted one room?"

Her tone had gone distinctly cold.

"With two beds." There was a hard edge to Grayson's voice. He wasn't trying to hide his anger anymore.

Wyatt just hoped they weren't about to get thrown out, or, worse, have the police called on them.

The woman's mouth was set in an angry frown as she typed them into the computer, took Grayson's credit card, and handed over the keys.

"Room eighty-three."

Grayson gave them one of the keys and pocketed his wallet. "Shall I drive us around?"

Wyatt shook their head. "I'll walk. I need to stretch my legs."

Room 83 was toward the end of the long, low building. Wyatt unlocked the metal door. The room sported twin beds, a small table by the window, a desk with a TV, and a bathroom. It had that vaguely musty, closed-in smell Wyatt associated with motels.

With a sigh, they sat on the edge of one of the beds. After a minute or two, Grayson pushed the door open and set the bags on the floor between the beds.

"Thanks for getting those." Wyatt stood. Grayson shrugged.

"Two overnight bags was no big deal. What were your plans for dinner?"

"There's this Italian restaurant that gets good reviews. It's not fancy or anything, looks like a hole in the wall, but ... I figured Italian would be good."

"Yeah." A small smile tugged at the corners of Grayson's mouth as he looked up at Wyatt. They were standing close now, close enough that Wyatt could look down and see the long sweep of Grayson's eyelashes against his pale cheeks. Wyatt was very aware of their height.

"Good." Wyatt distracted themselves by looking down at their phone. "Uh, just give me a minute, yeah? To check up on my mom?"

"I'm sure she's fine." Grayson reached out to take Wyatt's hand. "It's just the one night."

Fuck. Wyatt felt their throat close. They didn't want to ruin this night, but they had no idea how to answer that with anything but the truth. "She is most of the time. But she has Alzheimer's, so she's not as functional as she once was."

Grayson's expression changed immediately. "I'm sorry, that's … that must be hard."

"It's harder for her than me, of course, but yeah, it's hard."

They stared at each other. Grayson was still holding Wyatt's hand, and he gave it squeeze. "Go call. Then we can go to dinner."

Everything inside Wyatt seemed to soften, tension leaving them without support and briefly without mooring. At this point, they expected pity when they told people, and that dug deep into them because their mother was great, the best mother on the face of the earth, and no one should ever, ever *pity* them for loving her.

Grayson wasn't watching Wyatt with pity. There was no real understanding of the day-to-day life of living with someone with Alzheimer's disease, either, but at least there was no pity. Just a kind of acceptance.

"Thanks." Wyatt gave Grayson's hand a squeeze back and then went to make the call.

They called Jess's number in the chilly evening air, standing on the curb outside their motel room.

"Hey, Wyatt."

The cloud of worry that always hung at the back of their mind lifted a little at how calm she sounded. "How's Mom?"

"Fine. We went over there this morning, and we'll be over there tomorrow. She was okay this morning, you know, not great, but okay."

That brought the worry back, even though Wyatt knew it was irrational. There was nothing they could do, and Jess had said she was fine. "All right. Just call me if anything happens."

"Of course I will. Now go have fun doing your history thing." Jess's tone was encouraging and a little teasing.

It made Wyatt smile and then breathe out a small, relieved sigh, a puff of warm air evaporating into the night. "I'll try."

"Good." On the other end, Jess hung up.

Grayson was sitting on one of the beds flipping through TV channels when Wyatt returned.

"You're ready to go out?" Wyatt tried to set aside any lingering worry. "Or you need a few more minutes?"

"No, I'm ready now." Grayson clicked off the TV and stood. "How's your mom?"

"My sister says she's fine. She and her fiancé are keeping an eye on her." Wyatt busied their hands with making sure they had their wallet, phone, car keys, and room key tucked into their pockets.

"Good." Grayson nodded toward the door. "Come on, let's get some dinner."

The restaurant looked tiny from the outside, but also white and clean, and inside was rather classy, with couples dining together at small tables and art-work on the walls.

A smiling young woman approached them. "Just the two of you tonight?"

Wyatt nodded.

"Right this way."

She seated them at one of the little tables, put menus down for them, and bustled away to get water.

"What do you think?" Wyatt scanned their menu. "The beer-battered shrimp is supposed to be good here."

Grayson was frowning. He looked as if he was about to say something important, so Wyatt put his menu down and waited.

After a moment, though, he just shook his head and picked up his own menu. "The Alfredo looks good."

"Yeah." Wyatt reminded themselves that if it was important, Grayson would tell them when he was ready. "You want to split a serving? We could get Alfredo and the battered shrimp."

"Sounds good." Grayson set aside his menu.

Wyatt ordered when their server came back with water. They let their foot nudge Grayson's under the table, just a small touch of the toe of their boot against Grayson's. Their knees brushed Grayson's knees when they scooted forward. Grayson smiled at them, and they smiled back.

The silence that gathered between them was comfortable and warm. Wyatt didn't feel the need to interrupt it with chatter, and Grayson seemed just as happy to let it remain, as well.

"I've been reading a book," Grayson said after a while. "About portrait photographs and how they're being used now to reinsert marginalized people back into our understanding of history. People of color, mostly, there's been a real tendency to ignore portraits that were taken of nonwhite people both as historical sources but also as art, but that's starting to change." He leaned forward, and Wyatt leaned in, too. Close enough for their hands to almost touch. "Fredrick Douglass sat for more photograph portraits than any other person at the time, because he believed it was important for white people to see what a well-dressed, well-respected black man looked like. It's sad that these kinds of photographs have been ignored as a historical source. But also I thought it was interesting to see what other people are doing with them."

"You should send me the title of the book," Wyatt said. "I would love to read it."

"I can lend it to you once I'm done." Grayson leaned back in his seat again, putting a safer distance between them. "If you'd like."

"I would like that." Wyatt missed having Grayson close and wanted to reach out and touch his hand but kept their hands to themselves. The two of them lapsed into that easy silence again.

Their food came, and they arranged the huge plates between them and ate.

Grayson finally pushed his empty plate aside. "I wish I could cook like that. Heating premade food is about all I can handle, though."

"I wish I had time to cook and bake more. I enjoy it a lot, but work takes up most of my time these days." The way Grayson focused only on them when they talked made them feel a little shy, a little unsure. "Maybe I should have you over for dinner sometime. It would give me a reason to cook."

"I'd like that." Grayson smiled, and his gaze when it met Wyatt's was open and warm.

The server came with their check.

"Do you want to split?" Grayson was already taking out his wallet.

Wyatt shook their head. "Let me."

To their surprise, Grayson didn't argue, just nodded and put his wallet away.

The air was cold enough to make their breath cloud as they stepped out of the restaurant.

The sky had turned dark, deep blue, with threads of clouds that appeared much darker.

"You know what I want?" Grayson said from the passenger's seat.

"What?"

"Ice cream." Grayson gave Wyatt a look that clearly said, *And what are you going to do about it?*

Wyatt smiled. "I think we're going to pass a grocery store on our way to the motel. We can stop there."

The store was more like a mini-mart than a full grocery. Grayson swept in like he owned the place, ignoring the looks they got from the lady behind the counter and the men in hunting camouflage arguing by a Doritos display.

There was a small cooler of ice cream, mostly Perry's. "What about coffee ice cream?" Grayson asked, pointing to one with coffee pieces.

Wyatt shook their head. "I can't have coffee anything this late."

"Okay." Grayson pulled out a carton of chocolate-covered toffee pieces and pecans. "Can you do pecans?"

"Pecans should be fine." Wyatt just wanted to pay for the ice cream and get back to the motel—if for no other reason than that the two of them were still being stared at.

To Wyatt's relief, the group of men left before they got the ice cream up to the counter. The woman behind the counter didn't look pleased, but she let them pay without any hassle.

At the motel, Wyatt parked in front of their room and climbed out into the chilly night air. Grayson didn't move from his seat, but looked up.

Wyatt looked up, too, and saw the stars were out—small, pale, and watery in the night sky.

The motel sign sputtered on and off and on and off again. Wyatt stuck their hands into the pockets of their coat to keep warm and shuffled their feet across the cracked, uneven pavement. Above them, the sky was cloudy, the closeness of the town dimming the starlight. It was probably not what most people thought of when they talked about the beauty of the night sky. Here and now, though, with Grayson, Wyatt thought it was beautiful.

They stayed there until Wyatt's hands were cold even tucked into their coat, and then they turned toward the room. "We should go inside."

Grayson sighed, not a sad sound but one filled with such incredible longing. Wyatt wanted to walk around the car and touch him, pull him close and hold him, or even just take his hand.

They didn't, though. People could be watching from the motel rooms—like the woman at the front counter—or cars could pull in.

Grayson looked away from the sky, back at Wyatt, and nodded. "Yeah, we should."

Inside the room was like a sauna. The heat caused an unpleasant, stale smell to rise from the carpet.

They pulled off their coats and piled them on one of the beds.

Grayson's hair was rumpled, curls a little wild around his face. His cheeks pink from the sudden heat. He rubbed his hands together and sat on the other bed.

"Come on." He waved Wyatt over to the bed. "Let's eat some ice cream."

"I hope you like it." Wyatt liberated their spoon from its plastic wrapping. "We have a whole carton to eat before it melts."

"That's all right, I can eat my fair share of ice cream."

The two of them sat on the bed, the ice cream carton between, and ate in silence for a few moments.

It felt comfortable like that, sitting with Grayson, just hanging out. The whole day had been comfortable and sweet.

Finally, Wyatt reached out. They cupped the back of Grayson's head and pulled him close, and they kissed, all sweet and sticky, all toffee and pecan. Grayson's hands gripped Wyatt's shoulders, stroked up their neck, touched the hair at their nape with fingers that shook a little bit, drifted back down. Wyatt kissed him at the corners of his mouth, kissed his lips and then pulled away. "Do you want to do something? While we finish off the ice cream. Because I'm afraid if we get distracted now ..." Their gaze drifted down to Grayson's mouth. "It'll melt and make a mess."

"Do you want to watch something?" Grayson looked across the room at the TV.

"Sure." Wyatt slid off the bed before Grayson could and crossed the room. He flicked on the TV. The television didn't have a remote, and most stations were just static, but he found a station showing *Star Trek* reruns.

"You mind?" He turned to Grayson.

"We can watch this. It's been a while since I've seen *Star Trek*." Grayson settled himself more comfortably, so Wyatt left it on and sat back down on the bed.

They propped themselves against the headboard, the carton of ice cream between them.

Wyatt didn't think they'd seen *Star Trek: The Original Series* since they were a kid. They were surprised to find the episode stood up to adult watching as long as you were fine with special effects and props that looked like they came out of someone's garage.

The best part, though, was Grayson.

He giggled, and when Wyatt looked over at him he had a hand over his mouth, eyes brimming with mirth. Wyatt put the carton of ice cream with their spoon still stuck in it on the bedside table. Then they took Grayson's face between their hands. One of Grayson's hands fisted in the front of Wyatt's sweater. Grayson kissed them, just a press of lips at first, quick, small things that turned long and slow. Wyatt's fingers traced the shape of Grayson's waist just above his belt. They brushed underneath Grayson's shirt, pulled it out from his trousers.

In the background, the TV still played. Wyatt watched for a moment as Grayson began to strip off his clothes before fumbling with their own jeans.

Grayson was naked now, and Wyatt got totally distracted by the feel of Grayson's skin on theirs, the way Grayson felt in their arms and the weight of him against their chest.

Their hands ran down Grayson's body as the two of them kissed again, feeling down his sides.

They skimmed lower, hands shaping the curve of Grayson's ass.

Grayson kissed Wyatt's shoulder and turned them both so that Wyatt was on top of him.

"This going to be okay?" One of Grayson's hands came to land on Wyatt's chest.

"Yeah." Wyatt brushed their fingers along the side of Grayson's face, tracing the shape of his jaw. "We're going to be okay."

Grayson's head bent, lips tracing the line of Wyatt's collarbone, a light brush of his mouth, his breath moving against Wyatt's skin in a shaky sigh. He kissed down Wyatt's chest. Wyatt's hands rested on Grayson's shoulders, just holding on, letting him know it was okay. When Grayson kissed the seam of Wyatt's thigh, Wyatt took a long breath. "Yes. Yes, please."

"Tell me what feels good." Grayson's voice was a little bit pleading, a little breathless, words coming hot against Wyatt's skin, making them squirm.

"Okay," Wyatt said, even though everything Grayson was doing and had done was all warmth and softness and goodness and home. There was desperation around the edges, too, when Grayson touched them with his fingers and mouth, and Wyatt's whole body shook with it.

They pushed forward, fingers tangled in Grayson's hair, trying to hold on and ground themselves against the want and pleasure that was right there, pushing into the edges of their consciousness, filling them up. Grayson's mouth was sloppy and wet against them now, and Wyatt struggled to prop themselves up on one shaking arm, the other hand resting on Grayson's shoulder. They watched the way Grayson's hands moved, the tilt of his chin, the way light played against his face. Those long lashes dipped. Grayson's lips were swollen and so soft, open against them—to them.

Grayson's gaze flicked up, caught Wyatt watching, smiled, and his fingers twisted, strong and sure. Wyatt came, falling back against the bed, fingers tangled over their face. Grayson sat up, too, pried them away, and kissed Wyatt's still gasping mouth. He tasted of warmth and home, and Wyatt chased it with everything in them until Grayson was the one lying back against the bed with Wyatt bent over him. Their fingers ran down Grayson's body, feeling the little bit of softness around his belly up to the softness of his chest and then back down.

They touched Grayson between his legs, and Grayson sucked in a sharp breath, his fingers closed tight around Wyatt's wrist. "Don't ... not inside." His gaze locked with Wyatt's. "I'm not ..."

"It's okay." Wyatt leaned forward and kissed Grayson's lips, long and slow, kissed the side of his jaw and down the curve of his neck. "I understand, it's okay." They moved down Grayson's body, kissing and touching and hoping Grayson knew every one meant *please, please, please* ...

Grayson said, "Yes, yes, yes." Like he heard it and understood.

He went rigid when Wyatt parted his thighs, though, and then bent over him. Grayson gasped, and his arms moved as if he wanted to grab at Wyatt, then dropped to the bed.

"Oh, God." Grayson tipped his head back, looking at the ceiling.

Wyatt used their mouth and tongue and listened to Grayson gasp above them, making small keening noises Wyatt took to mean what they were doing was good.

It was certainly different, but not as different as they'd imagined—all warm, damp skin, and the taste was the same.

"Yes." Grayson's hand came down, pulling Wyatt forward, not pushing them away, and that Wyatt understood. "Yes, keep on doing that, just like that."

They licked and sucked and switched to using their fingers when that didn't seem quite enough to tip Grayson over the edge.

Grayson's hands left Wyatt's shoulders to clutch at the bed. His eyes had darkened to the color of fir trees, his mouth open and panting, and when he came he shook like he might come apart.

Wyatt crawled to lie beside Grayson.

"Well." Grayson laughed a little, and Wyatt smiled in return. Grayson rolled over and put his arms around Wyatt's chest, snuggling close, to Wyatt's surprise.

Wyatt arched their eyebrows. "Snuggler?"

"Yeah, I am." Grayson kissed them and then pushed at their shoulder. "Now roll over so I can spoon you."

Wyatt couldn't help it, they laughed. "You're a little small to be the big spoon." But they rolled over anyway.

"Fuck you, I'm not small." Grayson's arms went around Wyatt's waist, strong, and his body was warm against Wyatt's back.

As it turned out, Grayson fell asleep first, making a little huffing, snoring sound, still holding on around Wyatt's waist.

Wyatt fell asleep smiling.

CHAPTER 8

Of course, the two of them were in need of a shower in the worst way when they woke up. Wyatt stood and staggered to the bathroom. They washed and found Grayson was up by the time they came out.

He'd dressed in pajama pants and an oversized T-shirt with Wonder Woman on it. There was a Styrofoam cup of what must have been the instant coffee the motel provided in one of his hands, and his hair was a mess of curls falling into his face.

"Shower's all yours." Wyatt bent to kiss him good morning. Grayson's lips were soft, and he tasted like sweetness and cheap coffee. Wyatt wouldn't want it any other way.

"Good morning." Grayson smiled on his way past to the bathroom.

Wyatt got dressed, packed up their stuff, and threw away the ice cream carton.

Grayson came out of the bathroom dressed, his hair wet from the shower. "You ready to go?" Wyatt asked.

Grayson nodded. "Let's go."

The drive back to Grayson's house was quiet, the silence between them like the sunlight flooding into the car: warm, soft, and unhurried.

It was snowing when Grayson woke up Saturday and went into the kitchen to start his coffee. The snow was coming down in big, fluffy flakes from a slate gray sky, already blanketing the field across the road from his house.

The crows were back on his tree, hunched against the cold. Grayson figured they could stay.

Wyatt and he had made plans for Wyatt to come over today. So he texted Wyatt to see if they had any concerns about the weather.

It doesn't seem like it's snowing that hard, Wyatt texted back. *I'll be fine.*

Grayson dressed and moved around the house, cleaning and straightening it up so it would be nice for Wyatt.

Outside, the snow had gotten heavier, the sky dark, streaked with long clouds like scars.

He put the teapot on the stove and made himself a cup of tea.

The roads would be bad, especially up where he was, and Wyatt would be driving.

He wanted to text Wyatt again, but if Wyatt was driving, their phone would be off, or at least it should be.

Tea in hand, Grayson paced the length of the trailer and then back again. God, what if something had happened? People crashed all the time in the winter on roads like these. People died on roads like these. Grayson checked his phone, but Wyatt hadn't texted him again.

The snow was now deep enough to hide the dried grass of the yard and the gravel of the driveway.

Grayson sat on his couch and drank his tea.

The snow stopped, the clouds slowly chased each other across the sky, and the sun came out. When he heard the crunch of wheels against gravel, Grayson jumped and almost ran to the door.

Wyatt climbed out of their car in a dark blue and green plaid ankle-length wool skirt, boots, a pea coat, and aviator sunglasses.

"I was worried it snowed too hard." Grayson came halfway down the steps, heedless of the snow and his socked feet.

"The road was a little slick, but it was fine." Wyatt met him and pulled him into a hug. "It was fine."

Grayson leaned back to look up at Wyatt. "Yeah?"

"Yeah." Smiling, Wyatt kissed him on the lips.

"Well, come in." Grayson stood aside and watched Wyatt step into his house and pull off their boots and coat.

He didn't really know what to do with his hands, and Wyatt was standing there. This close, Grayson had to tip his head up to look at them. Wyatt really was terribly tall, and it had been a long, long time since he'd felt like this about someone. "You look really nice." Grayson cringed a little internally at how stupid he sounded. He reached forward and took Wyatt's hands between his and gave them a squeeze. "So." He cleared his throat and let Wyatt's hands go. "Tea? Coffee?"

"Are you drinking coffee?" Wyatt was doing that thing where they hunched, probably to appear shorter, which was endearing and made Grayson want to reach up and pull them down for a kiss.

"I was drinking tea, actually." Grayson decided the living room would be more comfortable for them both to settle than the kitchen.

"I'll have tea too, then." Wyatt followed him into the living room, and Grayson sat them down on the couch.

While the water heated, Grayson rummaged through the cupboard until he found a mug that didn't have something comic-book- or history-related on it, just red and black flowers.

"Black tea, or I have some mint, too?" he called.

"Black is fine."

"Here." He carried the mug into the living room and put it in front of Wyatt.

"Thanks." Wyatt took a sip as Grayson settled beside them.

"How's work been?" Grayson cupped his mug between his hands.

"Fine." Wyatt took another sip and settled back against the couch, long legs crossed. "What about you, what do you do when the historical society is closed?"

Grayson looked down at the floor. "I work at Schroder's supermarket."

"Oh, so how's that been?"

Grayson studied Wyatt's face, trying to tell if Wyatt thought less of him or not. "I mean, as good as it could be, I guess."

They were both silent for a moment, and Grayson glanced out the window at the snow and forest behind his house. "Hey, you want to go for a walk?"

"What? But it's snowed?"

"Yeah, but we could still walk." Now that Grayson had thought of it, he wanted to go, to do something with Wyatt he'd never done before, like a tiny adventure. "It's not even an inch out there."

Wyatt hesitated for a moment and then set their mug aside. "Sure."

Outside, the world was glittering white in the pale sunshine.

The soft snow under their feet muffled any noise they might have made.

The crows had gone, leaving the tree with bare gray branches reaching for the sky.

The field across the street looked like it had been tossed with handfuls of stars, all shining in the sunlight.

Grayson turned them away from the road, toward the woods behind his trailer.

The trees here were mostly pine. Green and dark, they whispered to each other as Grayson and Wyatt pushed past them. The ground behind his trailer had been white with snow, but between the trees it was still brown with fallen pine needles and rotten leaves. There were hints of gray where stone poked out of the earth and green from tiny round plots of moss. Some of the trees had lichen on them, too, green-gray feathering fish scales winding along the trunks.

"It's beautiful out here." Wyatt had their hands stuffed into the pockets of their coat. "It reminds me of when I was a kid."

He remembered Wyatt saying they'd grown up on farm outside the city. "Did you have woods on your land?"

Wyatt nodded. "And a little creek Jess and I used to play in during the summer."

"Yeah? My grandmother's house was the same, creek and everything."

It wasn't really a forest where they stood as much as a crop of trees, but it was quiet under the branches, a little dark, too. Grayson listened to small animals rustling through the leaves and the *tink, tink* of a woodpecker somewhere above them and to their right.

He walked, trying to keep his footsteps soft in the leaves, and Wyatt followed him.

They stepped out of the tree cover, finally pushing aside branches to see a field behind, a small hillside covered in untouched snow, and more trees beyond that.

"Do you know where your property line ends?" Wyatt asked.

Grayson shook his head. "I don't." But he stepped onto the untouched snow anyway.

Wyatt stretched their long legs and caught up with him, taking Grayson's gloved hand in theirs. Grayson looked up at them for a moment, surprised, but Wyatt just smiled.

They walked hand in hand across the snow, and now that they were on the hillside Grayson could see it wasn't as untouched as he had thought.

There were tracks back and forth—large ones that looked like a coyote or stray dog, smaller ones from a cat or something like it, and tiny long thin ones he had no idea about.

It occurred to him that in the last four years he'd lived in the trailer, he'd never been back here. Never gone behind the little backyard, in fact, when he went behind the trailer at all.

"We should probably turn back." Wyatt's big hand was warm around Grayson's. "If you don't know where your property ends. We don't want to trespass."

"Well, I guess you're the expert."

Wyatt laughed. "I do family law, not criminal law." They smiled down at Grayson.

"Come on." Grayson turned them back toward the trailer. "I can make more tea for us when we get back in, or hot cocoa."

"Cocoa would be nice."

They left their tracks in the snow, much like the other animals that had already been there. The wind had picked up, drawing the snow in little waves and gusts around their feet. It clattered through the branches of the pine trees.

Grayson opened the front door to his house. They stripped off their coats, boots, and other things, and Grayson led the way to the kitchen.

Wyatt looked a little odd in Grayson's space, leaning against one of the age-yellowed counters as Grayson searched through the cupboard for the hot cocoa mix. "I don't have any." He turned to Wyatt. "I'm sorry."

"Do you have baking cocoa, milk, and sugar?" Wyatt unfolded their arms and came to stand behind Grayson, looking over his shoulder.

"Yeah." Grayson dug the stuff out and gave it to Wyatt.

"Where're your pots?"

"Down by your legs." Wyatt knelt and pulled out a small pot. They put the pot on the stove and started measuring sugar and cocoa powder into it while Grayson got the milk.

"A little bit of vanilla and cinnamon's also nice." Wyatt added the milk, whisking the ingredients together as they did.

Grayson shook his head. "I don't have that. I don't do a lot of baking."

"It's fine." Wyatt gave him a smile. "It'll be good without it, too."

Wyatt stirred until steam rose from the dark surface of the cocoa.

Grayson took out two mugs from the cupboard. There were no normal ones left, so he bit the bullet and pulled out a mug with Tolkien's Elvish on it and another with happy-looking hipster men in ugly Christmas sweaters holding hands in a circle around it.

He was going to have to buy grown-up mugs one of these days, Grayson thought, taking the Elvish cup for himself after Wyatt poured steaming-hot cocoa into it.

They carried their cups into the living room, and Grayson cleaned away their short-lived tea. The hot cocoa Wyatt had made was darker, richer, and a lot less sweet than what Grayson was used to, but good nonetheless.

"So about Liam." Wyatt settled themselves on the couch, curled into one of the corners. "Have you heard about his military record yet?"

Grayson sighed. "No, but look, records from that long ago are sketchy. We might not be able to find anything."

"That's what you keep saying." Wyatt took a sip of cocoa. "But we keep finding things."

"I'm just saying there's not a single archive I can just go to and punch in his name." Grayson watched the stream rise off his own cup. "I want you to be prepared for when we hit a dead end, because we will sooner or later."

"I think you're being too pessimistic." Smiling, Wyatt reached over to squeeze Grayson's knee. "We will find them, you know."

They were silent for a moment.

"What if Liam and James were a couple?" Wyatt's face had gone serious now.

"What if they were?"

"Well, wouldn't that be interesting? An interracial same-sex couple? In like, what, early-nineteen-hundreds Upstate New York?"

"It would be." He couldn't think of any published research that existed at the moment about a couple like that, not for so early, not for the U.S., and certainly not for a town as small as Binghamton. It could be big news, actually, depending on what they had and what was done with it.

"We'd need sources we don't have to do that kind of research. I mean, the way queer history is done right now, we'd need a letter or a diary really laying out that their relationship was sexual and romantic—nothing less."

"That's a little homophobic, isn't it?" Wyatt frowned. "That it takes pretty much a signed confession?"

"And sometimes not even that's enough." Grayson blew across his cocoa, watching the little ripples spread across its dark surface. "It is homophobic. And you know, even when we do have letters or diaries, sometimes it comes down to questions like did their genitals touch, when, or in what way? It's bad, it's true, but that's just the way queer history is done in the U.S. at the moment."

Grayson watched Wyatt think about that—the problems and implications of it. "But what if they were in love but never physical?"

Grayson shrugged. "There's no real way to prove emotions like love unless it's written down—like, if there was a love letter. Otherwise, you could never prove it. There are plenty of late-nineteenth- and early-twentieth-century photographs of men being affectionate—tender, even—and it doesn't matter. It's about what you can prove."

Grayson thought for a moment, realizing something that had always been in his mind but he'd never spoken aloud. "There's no room in queer history for same-sex romantic love or intimacy that isn't also *provably* sexual."

"And they don't do that for straight couples?"

"No."

"So what if we did it differently?"

"How so?" Grayson was already thinking about it, though—the logistics of it and theory behind it.

"I don't know, what would you do if they were straight?"

"Well, with this photograph, nothing much." Yet at the same time, maybe just working with the photograph would let them push it farther. "But probably start from a position of assumed heterosexuality."

"So if we started from a place of assumed homosexuality?" Wyatt put down their cup and sat sideways on the couch, their attention fully fixed on Grayson now. "Hell, what if we threw cisgender out the window, too?"

Grayson had to work hard not to snort boiling cocoa up his nose. He sputtered until Wyatt took the cup away from him, looking concerned.

"Uh." Grayson licked his lips and thought about it. "Well, if we were working from the premise that they could be together, or they could not be cis, and then backward, we'd need to think about sources differently. I guess we could theorize the possibility of queerness or transness into our sources, specifically our visual sources."

He took a deep breath and let it out. It felt like he was about to step off a pier into very dark, very deep water. "We'd have to read this photograph differently. We'd be reading a guess about the moment this photograph represents and the queer possibilities within it, not using the photograph as a piece of proof for something else. So that the photograph isn't a piece of the puzzle—it becomes the puzzle, or maybe the frame with pieces that fit inside it. If that makes sense."

Wyatt had moved closer to him on the couch, listening with a kind of complete attention Grayson wasn't used to having aimed at him. His whole body ached with the academic implications of what they were putting together here. The possibilities this idea represented, what could be done with it. *Don't think about it, don't think about it.*

"Anyway." He reached for his cocoa and sipped it, not really tasting it anymore.

Wyatt was still mulling over the possibilities, Grayson could tell. They sipped their hot cocoa, thinking and thinking. Grayson hadn't ever met anyone who took this as seriously as Wyatt did and yet had no academic training at all. It occurred to him that Wyatt must be very good at legal research.

"Okay, so let's say we use the photograph to frame the conversation. Then what?"

"Well." Grayson tried to feel his way through unfamiliar territory. "That kind of photographic analysis isn't really done in history that often. So all of this is stepping into a realm ..." He made a motion with his hand like an aimless circle in the air. "Let's just say it would be new, but like we've talked about, 'proving' queerness or 'proving' transness is very difficult. I would be lying if I said I've never wondered if it was asking the wrong questions anyway. If we used something like a deep reading of a photograph, it could hypothetically reframe the conversation away from 'proof' and toward a queer or trans history that's more in line with what we expect from cishet history. What would that reading look like? I don't know. This is all new."

"I think part of what makes it attractive to me," Wyatt said, "is the fact that you don't know. Because, I mean, look at people—a lot of times you don't know if they're queer or trans. Look at me, I'm both, but I'm not out in a lot of ways, so if I lived a hundred years ago or even fifty years ago, would someone be able to point to my life and say, 'Yes, they were queer, they were trans'?" They took a breath, their hands shaking. Grayson reached forward and took Wyatt's hands in his own. Wyatt's gaze lowered to where their hands joined. "All I want ..." Their voice was soft. "... is the possibility that there is a space for people like me to exist in history too. To have a past. To look back with pride and say people like me lived and loved and endured. That's all I want."

A light came on in a dark room Grayson hadn't realized existed inside of him. He leaned forward until his forehead rested against Wyatt's shoulder. "Yes. I want that, too." More than that, he wanted to be the one who did the research, put down the words that made it possible for him and Wyatt. The hopelessness of it uncurled inside him. He was never going back, would never write or publish this. He was a minimum-wage worker with a degree that wasn't worth anything. Maybe one day someone would write this, but it wouldn't be him, and it wouldn't be for Wyatt.

Grayson hadn't realized he'd closed his eyes until Wyatt's fingers traced the skin just under each. "Don't be sad. We're going to do this, and we're together."

"I'm not sad." And that was such a lie.

"You looked sad before." Wyatt's voice was gentle, their gaze understanding.

Grayson looked away. "I was thinking about when I was in school, I used to be good at this, you know?"

Wyatt patted him again but remained quiet and still.

"When I was growing up here." Grayson looked down at his mug again, at the fingers curled around the outside of it. "I never knew anyone who could do this." He motioned between them. "What we just did. It was something special, something only I could do. It's so stupid and self-centered of me, but I had this idea in my head that I was going to do this forever, no matter what it took. I worked hard, and I sacrificed a lot ... I don't know." He came fumbling to a halt, unsure of what he was trying to say in the end, what point he was trying to make.

"I might be missing something here." Wyatt was frowning. They put their arm around Grayson. "But why can't you still do that?"

Grayson gave a little laugh. "It's been five years. No one remembers me enough to write me recommendations. Programs are going to wonder what I was doing all this time. I'll have to take the GREs again, and I don't have the almost two hundred dollars to do that. They say if you're serious about getting in, you need to apply to eight or more schools, and that'll be fifteen hundred to two thousand dollars in application fees and other stuff."

Wyatt looked a little stunned. Grayson's stomach was in knots just thinking about how impossibly big those numbers were.

"Right, I just don't make that kind of money, and what money I do make goes to paying off the student loans I have from my other degrees." Grayson swallowed, throat dry now. "I have a lot of student loans."

"I'm sorry." Wyatt's fingers rubbed small circles over the tensed muscles at the nape of Grayson's neck.

Grayson shrugged, not able to meet their eyes. "I did it to myself."

"I'm not sure you did." Wyatt pulled back and shifted on the couch so they could face Grayson again, reaching out and cupping his chin. "You came out, yeah? You had problems with your family? That's not your fault."

"No, I ..." Grayson finally looked up and met Wyatt's dark eyes, full of sympathy and caring. "I tried to kill myself," he said, spitting it out all at once before he lost his nerve. "After I came out, after my parents made it clear I wasn't going to be able to transition. After I'd realized I had to either stay with them or be homeless. I just ... I didn't even know what to do, I didn't have money, I didn't have a school to run off to, I didn't have friends I could call, I didn't have a job, I didn't ..." He stopped, because he'd run out of things to say. Instead, he curled his arms around himself, leaned forward. "I thought—I don't know what I thought. That it would work out, obviously."

"I'm sorry." Wyatt's voice was very soft. "I'm so sorry."

They put their arms around Grayson, gently guiding him out of his curled position to lean against Wyatt instead.

"It was a long time ago." Grayson's throat was sore, like he'd been crying or screaming, and he could feel the tears lodged behind his eyes. "I don't want to talk about this."

"Yeah." They were so close together he could feel Wyatt nod against his hair. "I get that."

It had started snowing again outside; Grayson could see through the window if he craned his neck.

"It looks bad out there." Wyatt's words were still soft and measured.

Grayson wanted to curl into the comfort of it, but also to put a little space between them, just so he could breathe.

"Well, stay as long as you want." He stood and picked up his empty cup to carry it into the kitchen.

Wyatt didn't follow him, and Grayson sighed as he turned on the water and washed out his cup. Outside the kitchen window, he could see the snow more clearly now, fat white flakes falling steadily and clinging together in clumps on their way down.

It was going to accumulate, maybe not even melt tomorrow.

He put the cup into the drainer and leaned against the edge of the sink.

"Hey." Wyatt had come to stand in the doorway between the kitchen and living room. "You okay?"

Grayson scrubbed one hand across his face. He was tired and a little bit upset. The truth was, though, that it had been a while. Wyatt was here, and neither of them was going to have to go out into the snow. All of that—it counted for something. "Yeah. I am." Wyatt came forward, shuffling across the linoleum in their socked feet, and put their arms around Grayson to pull him into a hug.

"Do you want me to make dinner?" Wyatt asked. "I know I promised you. And I'd love to, but I don't want to rummage through your fridge without your permission."

Grayson leaned his head against Wyatt's chest, let his eyes shut. "No, go right ahead, paw away. I'd love you to cook. If you're staying for dinner."

"I would love to stay, too. I'm not sure the weather is good enough to drive home anyway."

"I feel bad. I'm the host. I shouldn't be making you cook. But on the other hand, I can't cook, and you can."

"Don't worry about it, I'm perfectly happy cooking." Wyatt nodded toward the fridge. "Let's see what we have."

There wasn't a whole lot. Grayson wished he'd gone shopping before Wyatt came over, or at least brought some stuff home from work with him last night.

There was cheese, milk, eggs, a bottle of hot sauce, and a couple bottles of beer in the fridge, alongside a rather sorry-looking bunch of celery.

"Well," Wyatt said. "Why don't I make us mac and cheese, and I'll just throw in a lot of stuff for protein. I'll improvise."

"I have pasta. And there might be some sausage in the freezer, or hamburgers. Not very good stuff, I know." Grayson searched through the cupboards until he found the box of macaroni and put it on the counter for Wyatt.

"It's fine. Makes it more exciting for me, actually. Do you really have sausage? That'll be great in mac and cheese."

"Think so." Grayson rummaged through the freezer but couldn't find it. "Sorry, it doesn't look like there is any."

"It's fine." Wyatt came to look over Grayson's shoulder. "It'll be just as good without."

Grayson made a mental note to go shopping and make sure he actually had food before Wyatt came over next. He took a pot out of the cupboard and filled it with water for Wyatt.

He watched Wyatt move around the kitchen with a kind of ease Grayson never had in the space, taking things out of the fridge and putting the pot on the stove.

"Could you get the butter out for me?" Wyatt asked without turning around. Grayson got the butter out of the fridge.

It was interesting the way Wyatt spoke, their Upstate New York accent tinted by something else, something a little bit harder. Grayson had once had an Upstate New York accent, with the long, drawn-out 'a' and the tendency to drop the end off most words. He hadn't realized how pronounced it was until he'd gone to college. *Strong*, people had told him. Strong enough some couldn't understand what he was saying. And of course in other parts of New York there was a social and economic connotation to the Upstate accent: working-class and uneducated ... Grayson had flattened it out as fast as he could, though it meant having to say whole words now.

It was still pronounced in Wyatt's voice, though, the rocking cadences Grayson remembered from childhood and had gotten used to all over again these last few years. Except in Wyatt's case there was something else underneath. There was the hint of another accent that made Wyatt's vowels click together like beads as he talked.

"Were you born here, in this part of the state?"

Wyatt twisted around, surprised. "No, actually I was born up in the Adirondacks, but we moved down here when I was three. Why?"

"You have a north country accent." Now that he knew, it was obvious what it was turning Wyatt's 'cans' to 'kins' as they spoke.

"Do I? It's been so long since I lived that far north, but I guess that's where we lived when I learned how to talk, so some of it must have been absorbed."

"Yeah," Grayson said. "Yes, you do."

Wyatt smiled at him, full of life, love, and happiness in its rawest form. It settled inside of Grayson, soaking right into the core of him.

It was all right, Grayson thought. This evening, this moment, him and Wyatt. It was like what Wyatt had said. *They were going to be all right.*

"Come here." Wyatt turned from the stove and held out their arms. "Please."

And Grayson went, put his arms around Wyatt's waist, his face against Wyatt's chest, as Wyatt's arms curled around Grayson, holding him close.

Wyatt was warm and sturdy. They weren't holding Grayson tight, just enough for Grayson to know they were there, and that he was being held. "My cheese sauce is going to burn," Wyatt said after a long moment.

Grayson turned his face into Wyatt's chest and made a soft noise of disagreement, muffled by Wyatt's shirt.

"Come on, I want to eat dinner." Wyatt let go of Grayson. After a moment, Grayson sighed and stepped back.

"Is there anything I can do to help?"

"Sure, see if there's any vegetables aside from the celery we can have as a side." Wyatt was back to whisking the cheese sauce, so Grayson started going through the freezer.

"There's a bag of frozen peas." Grayson held them out. The bag was pretty old, but it was unopened, so he figured it was probably still good.

"Great." Wyatt took the sauce off the heat and pulled out another small pan. He dumped the peas in, added a little water, and put them on to warm.

Pulling open the fridge, Grayson dug out a bottle of beer. "You want one?"

"Yeah, sure." Wyatt didn't look up from the stove. "Not going to be driving tonight."

"Not tonight, huh?" Grayson tried to keep his voice as casual as possible.

He watched Wyatt freeze and then turn around slowly, blushing hard enough that their ears were red. "I mean, not if you don't want me to. I'm not try- ing to push you into anything or anything. It's totally up to you—"

"Stop," Grayson said before Wyatt fumbled it any more. "It's all right. I want you to stay." He held out the bottle.

Wyatt was still pink, but they reached out for the beer.

The macaroni and cheese ended up being baked with a little bit of bread crumbs on top and the peas cooked with butter.

They ate at Grayson's little kitchen table on the plates he'd inherited from his grandmother: white with tiny blue flowers.

"I'll do the dishes," Grayson said after they were done. "Since you cooked."

Wyatt helped move the dishes to the counter next to the sink as Grayson coaxed hot water out of the faucet.

"It's still snowing." Wyatt watched the snow fall out the kitchen window as Grayson washed pots, plates, bowls, and forks.

"It will probably snow all night."

Wyatt hummed agreement and picked up a dishcloth. He dried the dishes as Grayson washed.

Grayson liked how they moved together in the kitchen. There was something familiar about the way they brushed by each other. Their fingers touched when Grayson reached for a spoon, a tiny thing he felt through the entirety of his being.

Wyatt smiled at him and hung the cloth on the handle of the stove.

Grayson pushed himself onto his toes and kissed Wyatt on the lips, soft and gentle until Wyatt's hand came up to rest on the back of Grayson's neck.

They leaned together, and Grayson wanted— Wyatt's long-fingered hands, their tall frame, the way they smiled, and their obvious intelligence. He pressed himself into Wyatt, kissed them with intent and passion.

Wyatt touched him when they parted, traced the lines of his face, the curve of his neck, kissed him again.

"Come on." Grayson linked Wyatt's hand in his and pulled them toward the bedroom.

Wyatt followed him, easy and willing.

CHAPTER 9

Thanksgiving was coming, and every display of turkey-roasting trays, bags of stuffing, and canned pumpkin reminded Grayson of that fact. He'd asked Wyatt if they'd be spending their Thanksgiving with family. There hadn't been a lot of hope that Wyatt would be free, but Grayson had wanted to ask anyway.

"My mom and I will be going over to Jess's," Wyatt had told him, obviously apologetic. "But you could come, or rather I could ask Jess if you could come. I'm sure it would be fine."

"It's all right," Grayson had said. "It's family, I wouldn't want to intrude."

"Are you sure? They'd probably be happy to have you."

"Yeah, not my first Thanksgiving I've spent without family." Which was true, but even when he hadn't been able to come home he'd spent Thanksgiving with someone, a girlfriend or friends.

"Okay." Wyatt hadn't sounded all that sure, though.

Even though he wouldn't be eating dinner with Steve and the girls, Grayson decided he was going to make dinner anyway. He might not be as good a cook as Wyatt, but he could roast a turkey.

He started with the cookie dough.

Every time Grayson made a cookie tart, he used his grandmother's sugar cookie recipe. It was a very simple Pennsylvania Dutch recipe. He put the dough into the fridge to chill when it was done.

He peeled and sliced the apples and sprinkled them with a little bit of lemon juice to keep them from browning. Then he tossed them in cinnamon, cloves, nutmeg, and sugar.

He pressed his chilled dough into the tart pan and arranged the apple slices in a flower shape before pouring the last bit of juice over the top. The tart went into the oven, and Grayson got himself a beer and sat down to peel potatoes.

There was something very comforting about cooking. He wasn't good enough at it that he could think of other things while he did it. He had to keep his attention on the task at hand.

The scalloped potatoes went into the oven and the tart came out, crust very light brown, apples soft and caramelized in the sugar.

He rubbed the turkey with olive oil, salt, garlic, and thyme and started on the dough for the rolls.

He ate around three o'clock and then cleaned up and sat on the couch with the TV on, a movie playing.

The doorbell rang. Grayson pulled open the door to find Wyatt standing on the other side. Their hand was raised to ring the bell again. They held a wine bottle in their other hand.

"Hey." Wyatt looked down at Grayson.

"Hey. What are you doing here?"

"We ate really early." Wyatt stuffed their free hand in their coat pocket. "And my mom, she wasn't having an easy time, so she went home early, and I figured I'd come over here and see what you were doing." They held up the bottle. "I brought wine. It's a local Riesling. Well, it would be local if we lived up in Ithaca."

Grayson stood back. "Come on in."

Wyatt pulled off their coat and scarf. They wore a cute floral button-up with a lace knit shrug, a navy blue wool skirt, and wool tights. They pulled off their boots and hung up their coat while Grayson went in search of wine glasses.

He didn't have a whole lot of them left, although he did eventually find two from different sets.

"Do you want apple tart?" he called.

"That would be lovely." Wyatt came into the kitchen carrying the wine bottle. "Do you have a corkscrew?"

"Yeah, I do." Grayson pulled open the silverware drawer and handed it to them.

Wyatt opened the bottle and poured them each a glass while Grayson cut the tart. They carried their plates and glasses into the living room.

"This tart is so good," Wyatt said, stuffing a piece into their mouth. "So good."

"Thanks. It's my grandmother's recipe." Grayson picked up his glass of wine. "She used to make it sometimes for holiday dinner."

"It's great." Wyatt polished off their slice. "You're going to teach me how to do it sometime. That is, as long as the recipe isn't secret."

Grayson laughed. "It's not a secret. I'll teach you." He nudged Wyatt's shoulder with his own. "And thanks for coming over."

"It's no problem. It's nice, actually, good to take some time away, you know?"

"Is it—how is your mom doing?" Grayson wasn't sure if he should be broaching the subject.

Wyatt sighed and shook their head. "I know, I … you know, the temptation is to say she's fine, she's fine, but the truth is she's having a hard time. I think she's going to need to move to an assisted-living home soon, and God knows how we'll afford that."

"I'm sorry." There wasn't really anything else to say, was there? Grayson put his plate aside and moved closer to Wyatt on the couch, curling against their side. "I'm really sorry."

"Hey, not your fault, but yeah, it sucks."

They leaned into each other for a moment.

"You want another piece of tart?"

He felt Wyatt's body vibrate as they laughed. "That would be great."

The doorbell rang as Grayson padded by on his way to the kitchen. Frowning, he peered through the window on the door.

Steve stood on the other side holding a six-pack of beer, and Grayson was caught between bursting out laughing and maybe panicking a little.

He pulled the door open as Steve went to knock again. "Hey."

"Hey." Steve shuffled his feet a little awkwardly, looked at the ground. He was wearing his good jeans, work boots that had recently been cleaned, and one of his for-special-occasions-only flannel shirts under his battered Carhartt jacket.

"Let me guess," Grayson said. "Dinner finished up early."

"I, uh, kind of bailed, actually. Becca said she'd take the girls home. She was talking to Mary, church stuff, and I don't know ... I thought I'd come over."

"Bailed instead of watching football?"

Steve shrugged again. "Wanted to see how you were doing, thought I'd ..." He trailed off, looking a bit awkward, like maybe he was regretting that decision now.

That wasn't what Grayson wanted at all, because Steve bailing on Thanksgiving to find a place still selling beer and then coming out here in the cold was amazing, really. But at the same time, Wyatt was here. Grayson wasn't sure what to do. He just couldn't out Wyatt while they were sitting on the couch, eating tart, minding their own business.

"Grayson?" Wyatt called, and both Grayson and Steve froze for a second before Steve's gaze flicked up to Grayson's face.

Grayson didn't know what he looked like. Probably guilty.

"Or, you know," Steve said, trying to play it cool. "I could leave."

There was the padding of feet, and then Wyatt stood behind him, looking over his shoulder at Steve.

"Oh," Wyatt said.

Grayson had no idea what to do in this situation. He turned to Wyatt. "My brother, Steve."

"Hey." Wyatt reached around Grayson, hand extended. "Wyatt. It's good to meet you. Grayson's told me about you."

Steve did not say that Grayson had told him zero about Wyatt. Instead, he took Wyatt's hand and shook it. "It's good to meet you, too, Wyatt." When he let Wyatt's hand go, he looked awkward again. "I can take off, get back, they probably haven't noticed I'm gone yet."

"Oh, no," Wyatt said. "I mean, Grayson made tart, really good tart. Come in and grab some. You brought beer—yeah, it looks great." They stepped around Grayson, waving Steve inside the house.

"You sure?"

Steve was inside now, and Grayson nodded encouragingly at him. "Yeah. Join us for tart, and there are leftovers in the fridge."

He shut the front door and led the way into the kitchen.

"Uh, if this is a really weird thing to ask, just tell me," Grayson heard Steve say to Wyatt just behind him. "But what pronouns do you use?"

If he could have made himself die on the spot, Grayson probably would have, but Wyatt didn't seem at all fazed. "It's not weird," they said. "And I use 'they' and 'them.'"

Grayson was pretty sure Steve had never met anyone who used gender-neutral pronouns, but he just nodded and took the plate of tart that Grayson stuffed into his hands. He brightened visibly when he saw it. "You used Grandma's recipe."

"Yeah."

Wyatt helped themselves to another piece. "It is delicious. I've already made Grayson promise to give me the recipe."

Steve chuffed up a little bit at that. "Well, it is the best."

Grayson helped himself to a beer.

The three of them sat at the kitchen table with tart, wine, and beer.

"You have family local?" Steve asked.

Wyatt nodded. "All my family is local, lived in the area all my life, actually."

"Local." Steve nodded approvingly. "You, uh, you close to your family?"

"I'm very close with my mom and my sister," Wyatt said. "Not spoken to my father in twenty-seven years, but that's probably for the best. My sister and mom, though, we've always been real close." There was a brittleness to Wyatt's voice now. Steve didn't seem to notice it, but Grayson reached out, found Wyatt's hands folded in their lap, and braided their fingers together.

"We should play something," he said.

"Play what?" Wyatt turned to look at him.

"I don't know, board game, card game? Let me go look." He excused himself from the table. In the living room, he moved everything off the old sailor's chest he'd been using as a coffee table and opened it.

"We have history trivia games," he called into the kitchen. Both Steve and Wyatt groaned.

"You'll cream us at that," Steve called.

"I want to play a game I have a chance at winning."

Grayson wasn't sure if Wyatt had meant that for him or Steve.

"There are easy questions." Grayson pulled out a card. "Listen: *Was Plato a Greek or Roman philosopher?* See, obviously he was Greek, easy."

He bent to rummage through the trunk again.

"I didn't know that." There was a strong note to Wyatt's voice that Grayson had never heard before. Annoyance, maybe.

"I'm with them," Steve said. "I didn't know that either."

If history trivia games were out, then *Bethumped with History, Chronology,* and *Trivial Pursuit* weren't going to work. That left all of his role-playing books, which he hadn't touched in years, and a card game.

"Okay." Grayson pulled out the cards. "We could play this game about pirates."

"Pirates sound much better," Wyatt called.

"Yeah," Steve chimed in. "Let's go with the pirates."

He brought the game back into the kitchen, and Wyatt poured more wine for himself. Steve had another piece of tart in front of him.

"Do you want to be the red pirate, green pirate, or blue pirate?"

Wyatt inspected the cards. "Blue pirate. He's got a nice coat."

"Then I'll be the green pirate." Grayson took the card.

"Red pirate for me, then." Steve picked up the cards Grayson dealt him. "May the best, er, person win."

"That's not very piratelike of you." Grayson shuffled the deck. "I'm planning to cheat as often as I can."

It wasn't a particularly good joke, but Wyatt laughed anyway.

They played, only slightly hampered by the fact that none of the three of them was a hundred percent on the rules. The game seemed to involve a lot of blowing other people's ships up.

Wyatt played with an intense focus, eyes on the cards, seeming to forget their wine glass and tart. It was distracting to Grayson watching them bend over their hand, hair falling into their face, soft-lit by the light over the sink.

"I'm going to take the little ship to the right," Wyatt said, playing down a couple cards.

"Shit! No." Grayson's attention went back to the cards.

"Wait, what did you do?" Steve craned to see the cards Wyatt was laying down on the table. "I want to do that. Why do I only ever get the palm tree cards? What are they even good for?"

They all inspected a palm tree card.

"Food?" Wyatt offered eventually. "Water?"

"But not blowing ships up?" Steve said without much hope.

"Sorry." Grayson patted him on the back. "I don't think so."

Wyatt won, of course. Grayson's and Steve's forces were decimated, and they finally had to admit defeat.

Steve stood after they'd cleared the game off the table. "Thanks." He pushed his hands into his pockets again. "For all this."

"Thank you for coming." Grayson hugged him, which involved shuffling and back patting on both their parts.

"No problem. Really." Steve shook hands with Wyatt one last time.

He smiled and waved to them once outside in the snow, and Grayson listened to his truck start and head down the drive.

"So." He leaned against the counter, turning to Wyatt. "I'm sorry if I embarrassed you."

Wyatt shook their head. They turned on the tap and began washing dishes. "It's fine."

"You sure?" Grayson edged toward Wyatt and the sink.

Wyatt sighed, hands stilling in the water against a plate. "Sometimes I worry that I won't be able to keep up with you intellectually."

"Wyatt." Grayson moved closer, even though Wyatt was still not looking at him. "Think about the stuff with the photographs. You've done just as much as I have—more, because you didn't give up. You found Liam, and your interpretation of the photographs is stuff I could never do. I've never felt like you weren't keeping up." He reached out and put his hand on Wyatt's arm. "Education's not intelligence."

"I know that." Wyatt took their hands out of the water and shook them dry. "I just worry."

"You push intellectually and you think creatively, and I admire that so much." Grayson leaned forward to kiss Wyatt on the cheek. "So please don't worry about it. Please."

Wyatt nodded but didn't look wholly convinced, so Grayson kissed them again and then shoved them gently over. "Let me finish the dishes."

Grayson washed. Wyatt watched him for a while and then reached for a dishcloth. "Let me dry."

They worked in silence until the dishes were done and the leftovers put away.

"You okay?" Grayson took Wyatt's hands in his.

"Yeah." A little bit of the unhappiness that lingered in Wyatt's expression cleared. They smiled and bent to kiss Grayson. "Thank you."

"Come on." Grayson pulled them back into the living room, and they both curled on the couch.

"For Christmas"—Wyatt put their arms around Grayson—"would you come and celebrate with me and my family?"

"Steve might want me to celebrate it with him and the girls." Grayson leaned against them. "But if not, then yeah, I'll definitely come and celebrate it with you, your mom, and your sister. And even if Steve does want me over, we'll figure out a time."

It was a little bit of a commitment to say they'd be together at Christmas, but it was only a month or so. It felt pretty safe to Grayson.

None of this scared him now.

There was a large envelope stuffed into his mailbox when he pulled up to his house. Grayson parked and then walked back up the driveway to retrieve it.

Thomas Harris, the return address said. *Indiana University*.

Grayson brought the envelope into the house and put it on the kitchen table while he pulled off his coat and boots. He put the kettle on for tea and then sat down and opened the envelope.

A bundle of papers were held together with a paper clip. On top, a photocopied photograph. He sucked in a long breath. "You have got to be kidding me."

He took out his phone and texted Wyatt: *I got a package from the military history friend of mine, and you need to see the picture he sent.*

His phone buzzed seconds later with a text from Wyatt: *Just got off work, heading over.*

Grayson made his tea and read through the rest of the material Thomas had found for him.

He heard the crunch of wheels and was up before Wyatt rang the bell.

"You have got the see this." He waved Wyatt in and watched impatiently as Wyatt stripped off their outer clothes.

In the kitchen, Grayson slid the photocopy across the table to Wyatt.

"Oh." Wyatt reached for it. "Oh."

The photograph was of two young men, both in uniform but still very obviously James and Liam. They were posed together, sitting side by side, again neither smiling.

And even though the photograph was blurry, both because of its age and the photocopy, they could still see that Liam and James's hands were together, James's smaller hand on top of Liam's.

"So where does this put us?" Wyatt asked.

"I think that depends on what we're trying to do." Grayson sat at the table and folded his hands in front of him.

"Well," Wyatt said. "If we were to reframe the other photograph, like we were talking about, with assumed queer and transness, I guess having this one makes that easier?"

"I mean, yes and no. I think if we were to think about this traditionally, this is still not enough evidence, *but* I think for our purposes this is an amazing find. Not only does the fact that they served together in the army, probably met that way, give us more concrete information, but we can also do a reading of this photograph around physical touch and intimacy. Even if we wouldn't be able to argue that because they were touching they therefore identified as queer, we can argue the queerness of the moment that got caught here in the photograph. That's the thing that has always bothered me about photographs like this." Grayson had to stand up. He couldn't sit down anymore. "Remember when we talked about same-sex intimacy in photographs? The first time?"

"Yes, and you said it couldn't be used to prove queerness because straight men posed like that too sometimes." Wyatt leaned back in their chair.

"Yes." Grayson paced back and forth. "But here's the thing I've never been able to understand: why does that stand in the way of a queer reading? We have these incredible photographs, but we, as in queer scholars, can barely use them because they *might* be pictures of straight dudes?"

He could feel himself getting more worked up and more passionate as he talked. Wyatt was grinning at him.

"What?"

"Sorry." Wyatt ducked their head, still smiling. "I think you're right, and I like that you feel strongly about this."

"Oh." Grayson crossed his arms. "I'm glad we agree."

"No, no." Wyatt waved their hand. "Don't let me stop you. I want to hear the rest."

"Well." Grayson took a breath, trying to collect his thoughts again. "The thing is, I started thinking about it like this: after hundreds of years of having our history intentionally destroyed, we have to be the ones who step aside because maybe we'll call a straight guy queer? No, I don't think so. You know what?" He pointed at Wyatt. "You said, 'Isn't that homophobia?' and you were right. The more I think about it, the more I realize you're right, and it makes me angry."

"Okay." Wyatt laid one hand on top of the photocopy. "Let's do something new, then, like we've been talking about. Let's reclaim these photographs in the name of queerness."

That made Grayson laugh and sink back down at the table. "It's not going to be easy. The research alone could take a year. Even without a strict academic end goal like writing a journal article or book, still, to do it right is going to take a lot of work."

Wyatt smiled at him. "Good. Because I love this, I love being a part of it and watching you do it. I don't want to stop, not anytime soon."

Grayson covered Wyatt's hand with his own.

For a moment, they sat in silence, just holding hands, and then Grayson stood and went to the stove.

"Tea?" he asked.

"That would be great." Wyatt picked up the photocopy. "I was serious before, you know? How will this change the reading of the first photograph?"

"We could do a compare and contrast." Grayson filled his kettle and turned it on. "I always figure when you have two similar sources they're going to be compared anyway. Might as well be the one to do it. I think more so with photographs."

"One of the things I noticed the first time I ever looked at the photograph"—Wyatt shifted forward to gaze down at the new photocopy—"was that it felt candid to me. I can't point to anything or say, 'Well, the poses,' or do something someone like you would do, but to me it felt like the photograph had been caught the moment before the pose, if that makes sense. There was a rawness, I guess. I get the same feeling from this one."

Grayson poured hot water into two cups while he thought about the implications of what Wyatt was saying. "Do you want black tea or herbal?"

"Black is fine." They sat back in their seat to watch Grayson. "Anyway, that's just what I think."

"I want to hear more of what you think about this." Grayson leaned against the counter. "I'm serious, I really do. You said you think this one could be candid, too?"

Wyatt turned back to look at it. "Well, it feels like to me that this isn't the photograph they were paying someone to take. When you look at it, they're slouching a little bit, James looks like he's about to smile for once, Liam is holding ..." Wyatt leaned close to the grainy photocopy, close enough their nose brushed against it. "He's holding a cigarette, I think. They're about to get their picture taken, but they're not getting their picture taken, if that makes sense. To me, this makes the pictures even more special, because we have this moment that wasn't meant to be captured."

Grayson carried the two cups to the table and leaned over Wyatt's shoulder so he could study the image, too.

"I wonder sometimes if that was why they hid the first picture away." Wyatt looked up at him, gaze soft. "Not because they got their photograph taken together, but that somewhere the actual portrait existed and this was the one—the one where they weren't quite right or ready—that people weren't supposed to see. Maybe because it gave too much away, or maybe because there was just too much emotion there, too many memories."

"I wonder where this one is housed." Grayson picked up the photocopy. "I'm going to have Tom send me a scanned copy. So we can see it more clearly."

Wyatt shook their head, smiling, a little amused. "So practical, but yeah. I think that's a good idea."

"What you said." Grayson touched the soft hair at the back of Wyatt's neck. "About the candid qualities—I think it's important. I think it's where we should be focusing the analysis, and it's not something I would have thought of on my own."

Wyatt laughed at that, as if it had shaken them out of their thoughts. They leaned back in their chair, fingers curled around their mug of tea. "I know. But I like you anyway."

It was Grayson's turn to smile.

Grayson was in the store early to do prep the next day. He scooped out the cooled pasta and measured mayonnaise into it. He chopped the hard-boiled eggs and added them, too.

Wyatt was taking him out on a date tonight, and it made his heart speed up just thinking about it. It was going to be good. They were going to a brewery that Wyatt had scoped out already for possible queer and trans friendliness.

Grayson was going to wear his black button-down shirt with French cuffs, and he had some rhinestone cufflinks he hadn't worn since grad school. He had to think of what tie he wanted to wear, or maybe a bowtie.

Robert came into the back, pulling on his apron and coat. "Hey." He gave Grayson a friendly smile.

"Hey." Grayson smiled, too.

Robert stepped out into the store as Grayson added salt and pepper to the macaroni salad. He stirred the salad, and then Darleen and Robert came back and started rummaging through the fridge to take out the ingredients for the other salads. Darleen started on the potato salad, and Robert took out the coleslaw dressing and a big mayonnaise jar.

"You almost done with that?" Darleen asked Grayson without turning around.

"Almost." Grayson stirred it again, careful not to break up the pasta.

"When you're done, check up front." Darleen waved toward the deli case, and Grayson nodded.

"I can do it." Robert put his coleslaw prep aside on the counter, turning to head up front. "Grace doesn't have to."

"No, she can do it." Darleen crossed her arms, voice impatient. "She'll be done before you. Right, Grace?"

The words twisted inside Grayson, snapping him back from daydreams of clothes and a lover who actually respected who he was. It was like a wire being tightened one rotation too far. "No." His voice came out strong and clear, even if it felt like he was listening to it from a great distance. "Not she, *he*. Not Grace, I don't use that name anymore."

There was dead silence behind him, and Grayson turned slowly to face Robert and Darleen. They were both staring at him.

He was going to be fired. The reality of it settled onto him, but he still felt strangely calm.

"What?" Robert looked confused and unbelieving.

Or maybe he wouldn't be fired. Maybe they'd just ignore it and go on as if he had never said anything at all. The idea that he could come out and still be misgendered—he wasn't sure which would be worse.

Darleen took in a long, hissing breath, and Grayson braced himself, trying not to flinch. He flinched anyway.

"Well, why didn't you tell me before now?"

She turned away, shaking her head at his inability to trust her, and mixed mayo into her potatoes.

"What name do you go by now?" She'd turned back to him, expression aghast that there was yet more information he'd kept from her.

"Grayson." He tried not to fall on the floor with relief.

She nodded like she'd guessed it already. "You done with that salad yet?"

Grayson looked down at the bowl and then back at her. "Uh, yeah."

"Go out and fill the bowls for the case then." She waved him off, her tone now impatient that he hadn't thought to do this work already.

Grayson picked up the bowl of salad. His hands still shook ever so slightly, but he felt lighter.

CHAPTER 10

I t was Grayson's day off today, which meant he had to clean the trailer and do laundry before Wyatt came over in the evening.

Grayson staggered into his bedroom and dropped a huge armful of clothes onto the bed. He sat beside it, sorting out socks and trying to match them, then sorted the shirts that needed to go on hangers.

While his hands were busy, his mind kept circling back to the photograph. When he'd been in university, he hadn't done much original research. The master's students had not been encouraged to. Doing it would mean building a body of research that had never been done before. It would require professors to deal with sources they'd never heard of, new theoretical ideas, or maybe even new methodologies. That would mean extra work and time for faculty—work they tended not to want to waste on students only there for two years. *Don't stray off the beaten track* was the advice Grayson had gotten early on, so he hadn't.

He'd done queer history, but only when there was strong documentation—letters, diaries, court documents, and of course secondary sources. He might talk with Wyatt about creating space for other kinds of history, but he hadn't actually ever done that work. There were people, of course, who did, but Grayson had only talked to other students about that kind of research, while his own work tended toward the traditional.

There was a pleasure in working with someone's diary, their private letters. A type of voyeurism that came with actually putting your hands on documents that were once private, words written in secret.

Working with photographs was something altogether different: another kind of intimacy.

Grayson had known only one person who worked with photographs primarily. History was, as it had always been, a text-based discipline. Often, where there were no text sources, no history would be done.

Doing history with visual sources promised to be something different. Grayson had always figured he'd have time for that sort of experimentation when he was working on his dissertation.

"It's a very different thing," a professor had said once, talking about photographs as historical sources.

"Everything slows down when you work with photographs. There's a stillness to it, a quiet attentiveness. It forces you to really stop and see what's there."

Working with photographs was detail-oriented work. It was unforgiving in a lot of ways. Grayson really wished now that he had a background in it.

In a lot of ways, he'd been going about this research half-assed, mostly because it hadn't felt like *his*. It was something he'd done for Wyatt, because Wyatt had wanted to know. Even after he'd told Wyatt to give up, he'd still done research for them, because he'd wanted Wyatt to notice him, to think he was smart—to like him. Even after their failed date, he'd done it because he had something to prove to Wyatt, even if it was only in his mind.

So where did that leave him now that they were lovers? Without Wyatt in his life, would he still do this research? Or was it okay to do it for other people and not necessarily for himself?

That was another rule in historical academia: you always had to do the research for yourself, or you weren't going to make it. Let professors tell you what they thought you should be doing, but stand your ground at the end of the day and do what you wanted to do. Because once you got into dissertation-level original research it was going to be difficult, painful, unforgiving work, and it had to be for you.

He wasn't writing a dissertation, though, and Wyatt was part of this process, a partner in it. Maybe Grayson had started out doing this for Wyatt, but they were doing it together now. So maybe it didn't matter why he was doing it anymore.

He went over to his closet to get some hangers. As he reached for a handful, his foot ran into a box sitting on the floor. Grayson swore and dropped the hangers. There were a bunch of boxes, stuff he'd never unpacked after he'd moved in here. He'd forgotten how many there were.

Grayson dragged three of them out of the closet. The first one he opened was full of pictures in frames, bookends, and little trinkets. He pushed it aside and opened the next one, pulling out *The Straight State* by Margot Canaday, *Men Like That* by John Howard, *Gay New York* by George Chauncey, *Feeling Backward* by Heather Love, and others, all of them from school. The next box had extra dishes and kitchen supplies he didn't often use.

Sitting back, Grayson stared at the books, pictures, and pots and pans. It felt odd to have these things packed up and forgotten about in his closet. There were places in the living room for the knickknacks and books, and no good reason why he shouldn't have all his dishes in the kitchen. What if he wanted to invite more than two other people over to eat? What if he wanted to have Steve and Wyatt back again to play more board games or, God forbid, actually entertain?

But that was the thing, the reason the living room was bare of framed pictures, the kitchen set up for him to only have one guest at a time. He had never intended to stay here. The trailer was set up the way he set up his university apartment: with only the essentials unpacked, because he'd be moving soon anyway.

He'd lived here, by himself, for three years and had been out of school for five.

It was time he put some pictures up, for God's sake.

Grayson picked up the box of dishes and carried it into the kitchen. If he rearranged stuff, there would be plenty of room for the extra plates and bowls. And this way, if he had friends over, there would be no awkward digging through the closet for them. Even if he never needed more than two sets, the cupboard was as good a place as any to keep them.

On the counter, his phone started vibrating with a call from Bertha Murray. She served on the historical society committee and was one of the few members who liked him, so he picked it up. "Hello?" Grayson held the phone between his shoulder and his ear as he took a stack of serving bowls he never used out of the cupboard.

"Hello, Grayson, how are you doing?" Bertha started right in on the mandatory small talk that always preceded whatever she'd actually called about. "Staying warm with all this cold weather, I hope."

"I'm doing well." Maybe he could put the serving bowls down in the bottom cupboard. "And staying warm."

"Good. There's something I want to talk to you about." Bertha's tone had lost its brightness as she transitioned into the business part of the call.

Grayson froze. Was she about to tell him he'd been fired? Was this because he'd worked on the photograph with Wyatt during work hours? But how would she know that? Worse, was this about his being trans? Didn't they already know? He'd never directly come out, but he'd always figured since he'd applied under his chosen name and referred to himself as a man without actually totally passing, some of them had guessed.

On the other end of the line, Bertha sighed. "You know times have been hard for us. The historical society used to be open every weekday, but with our money troubles we had to limit our open hours to two days a week."

"Yes."

"Well, funding is, if anything, even tighter now, and Grayson, dear, we're meeting later this week to decide if we can keep the historical society open at all."

"Oh," Grayson said. There wasn't much else to say.

Bertha sighed again. "If we decide the money just isn't there, then you would have until the end of the year."

"Okay." Grayson put the dishes aside and sat at the kitchen table.

"So we'll see." She didn't sound hopeful, though. "But I thought you should know, and also I wanted to tell you that if we do decide we can't continue to keep the historical society open, it's not your fault. You've worked very hard these last few years, and we appreciate that."

"Thank you." If they shut down the historical society, then what? What would he do? He needed that money, and working at the historical society allowed him to still work in the field of history. Without it ... Working there even only twice a week had been keeping his foot in the door. It had proven he could still do the research, that his MA wasn't a complete waste of time and money.

Oh, God, what was he going to do without that extra paycheck?

"I'm so sorry." She sounded genuinely unhappy. Grayson tried to find something to say back and failed.

"Take care of yourself."

The line clicked off. Grayson leaned forward and pressed his forehead against the cool, scarred surface of his kitchen table. He was going to have to get another part-time job or pick up more hours at the deli. *Fuck!*

He sat up and pressed his hands over his face. It was just what he needed right now, to lose his job on top of everything else. Still, it could have been worse. This could have been his only job he was losing.

He stood and retrieved his phone. Wyatt's number was right at the top, the most called. He pressed it, listened to it ring and then go to voice mail, which made sense, Wyatt was probably at work. The knowledge didn't stop his heart from dropping anyway.

For a moment, he just listened to himself breathe.

"Hey." He forced himself to get the words out. "It's me. I just got off the phone with one of the historical society committee members, and, um, ... I think I'm losing my job." He took a long, shuddering breath, not trusting himself to say more than that without breaking down into tears. He pressed END.

He put the phone on the table and sat staring at nothing for several seconds.

Then he got up and went back to putting dishes away in the cupboard.

"I got your voice mail." They were out of their car and moving toward Grayson, who stood on his stoop, hugging himself against the cold.

Wyatt didn't hesitate. The moment they were within reach, they pulled Grayson into a hug.

"I'm so sorry." Wyatt pressed a kiss against the top of Grayson's head, and Grayson just wrapped his arms around Wyatt's waist and held on.

"I didn't know. That money was that tight, I wasn't prepared for this."

Wyatt sighed and rocked them both a little bit where they stood. "I'm sorry this is happening to you. It sucks, and you don't deserve it, not on top of everything else."

"No one deserves to have their job just evaporate from under them." Grayson leaned his cheek against the scratchy wool of Wyatt's coat. "But thanks."

They stood for a moment longer. Then Wyatt untangled themselves and pulled Grayson toward the house. "Come on. It's warmer inside."

It was warmer. Grayson kicked off his boots and shivered a little as the difference in temperature fully hit him.

Wyatt peeled off their own winter things. They'd come straight from work, Grayson saw, and were still dressed in slacks, a button-up shirt, an ugly tie.

His heart uncurled a little bit, and he reached forward, hand fisting in the cheap polyester of the tie, scratchy against his palm.

"Hey." Wyatt let themselves be pulled close, let Grayson smooth one hand across the cotton of their shirt, up to the stiff collar, graze his knuckles against the not-yet-warmed skin above it. Wyatt tilted their head, let Grayson lay his hand flat against the side of their throat, feel their pulse, the way the muscles moved when they swallowed.

Wyatt watched his eyes, but their hands were at their sides, just letting Grayson touch. Grayson's hand moved down from Wyatt's neck to the tie again, unknotted it, and pulled it free. Wyatt was still watching him, still not saying anything, mouth curved up into a small smile.

Grayson's fingers found the plastic button at the collar of Wyatt's shirt and pressed it through the hole, then dropped to Wyatt's hands. The cuffs were stiff there, too, and Grayson pushed the button of first one and then the other, feeling the give and the cuffs opening under his fingers.

Wyatt was still watching, quietly waiting. Grayson reached up, pulled just a little on their collar, enough to make Wyatt's head bend and bring them close enough to kiss. The kiss itself was a brush of lips, a barely there ghost of a thing, that made Wyatt's lips part, made them take a small step forward. They stopped when Grayson pulled back, though.

"What do you want?" Wyatt's hands were still at their sides, not depending, just asking.

Grayson sighed, not sure what it was he wanted. "I don't know."

Wyatt reached forward, then caught his hands, pressed them back against Wyatt's chest. Wyatt's skin was warm now. Underneath the cloth, their hands were warm, too. "Tell me how I can help you."

Grayson knew they didn't mean just in that moment, either, and he took another shaky breath. "Just be here. Just eat dinner with me, and sleep next to me and be here with me."

"Okay." Wyatt smiled down at Grayson, fingers tightening around his. "That I can do."

Grayson kissed them again, and then pulled them farther into the house.

CHAPTER 11

A buzzing noise cut through Wyatt's sleep. They rolled over onto their side and listened to it for a few moments before realizing it was a cell phone vibrating on the bedside table.

Grayson muttered something, voice heavy with sleep, and curled farther into the blankets, but Wyatt sat up, heart quickening.

Their fingers closed around the still vibrating phone.

JESS was displayed across the screen. Wyatt's breath caught, throat closing with the beginning of panic as they fumbled to bring the phone to their ear. "Jess?"

Please let everyone be safe.

"It's Mom." Jess's voice was too controlled.

Wyatt thought their heart would stop for a split second before they were moving, sliding out of bed, searching for their clothes. "What happened?"

Still in bed, Grayson sat up and switched on the lamp. "What's going on?

"She fell down the stairs leading up to her apartment." Wyatt closed their eyes in pain, thinking of that steep hundred-year-old staircase.

"Is she okay?" It was the only thing they could get out.

"I don't know yet. One of her neighbors called 9-1-1, and the paramedics called me. We're on our way to the hospital right now."

"Wyatt?" Grayson pushed the blankets back and got up.

Wyatt turned to him. "My mother's in the hospital."

"Oh, God." Grayson looked stricken. "What can I do?"

"I don't ..." Wyatt fumbled with the shirt they'd worn to work the day before, trying to get it buttoned one-handed. "Jess, what was she doing out of her apartment this late at night?"

"I have no idea." There was real fear bleeding into her voice now. "The paramedic I talked to said she was disoriented, although they didn't know if that was because of the fall or not."

"Shit." Wyatt stumbled out of Grayson's bedroom and into the hall, heading for the door. "Which hospital are they taking her to?"

"Binghamton General."

"Okay." Wyatt found their shoes. "See you in a few minutes."

"Yeah. You drive safe, okay? I can only deal with one family member in the emergency room at a time."

"I will, love you." Wyatt hung up and pulled their car keys out.

"Wait." Grayson had followed them, now fully dressed in jeans and hoodie. "Do you want me to come with you?"

"No, stay here." Wyatt yanked open the front door, greeted by a gust of snow. "I'll call you, okay?"

If Grayson answered, Wyatt didn't wait to hear before they ran for the car.

When they pulled up in front of Binghamton General Hospital, Timothy stood by the front entrance, his slender form bundled against the cold under a weak streetlight.

Wyatt navigated their car into the visitors' parking lot and walked up the sidewalk to where Timothy waited.

"Any news?"

"Jess was talking to the nurses that looked her over originally when she got here, and a doctor, I think," Timothy said. "But I don't know what's going on."

They walked into the hospital together.

Jess sat in one of the waiting room chairs, staring blankly at the opposite wall. She stood when she saw them. "Oh, thank God, Wyatt."

They went to her and gave her a hug. "What's going on?"

"She has a concussion for sure, and they think she's broken her ankle and maybe one shoulder bone. They're doing X-rays now." She hugged them back hard. "I don't know more than that. I saw her briefly, but she wasn't very lucid."

"She can't stay in her apartment if she can't walk," Wyatt said. Jess and Timothy exchanged a look.

"We've agreed she'll come and live with us, at least for a little while, but if she's falling down stairs and getting concussed we need to move her into an assisted-living home as soon as possible."

"I don't want her to go to any of the ones here. I handle those cases. I don't want to put her at risk like that."

"Then what about the one up by Ithaca?" Jess asked. "We both liked that one."

"Yeah." Wyatt sank down onto one of the hard vinyl-covered seats. Jess was right: the assisted-living home up in Ithaca was the only one in the area they trusted. They just didn't know how the three of them were going to afford it. It was an awful feeling, knowing she couldn't live on her own but the only two choices they had were assisted-living homes where Wyatt knew elder abuse happened or ones they really couldn't afford.

"When are we going to know what the X-rays tell us?"

Jess shook her head. "I don't have any exact time, but I know the nurses and some of the doctors here, so that should speed things up."

Wyatt put their face in their hands. They'd hoped, so much, that they'd have more time.

They heard the creak of the chairs next to them as Jess and Timothy sat. In the background, a TV droned on low, and behind that Wyatt could hear people walking back and forth, talking in low voices.

"I'll go out and get us all coffee and some food," Timothy said. "When places open, that is."

Wyatt flipped their phone over and saw it was 11:34 p.m. They put their head back into their hands.

Minutes ticked by, and when Wyatt felt like their fingers were pressing into the skin of their face hard enough to leave red marks, they sat up again. Nothing had changed; they were in the same dull waiting room with the same muted TV noise in the background.

Wyatt took out their phone to find it was ten after midnight, unlocked it, checked Facebook. They clicked on and read one of the articles someone had linked. The dullness of it, the ordinariness, was soothing.

The seconds and minutes crawled by. They put the phone back in their pocket and stood. They paced around the room, then examined the pile of old magazines.

They heard Jess get up and head off down a hall.

"Where's she going?"

"I think to talk to someone about your mom." Timothy scooted down in his seat so he could lean his head against the back of his chair and closed his eyes.

Wyatt sat as well but was too restless to try and sleep or even relax.

Jess came back a good ten minutes later. Wyatt walked to meet her.

"I've talked to her doctor," Jess said. "He said her ankle is broken for sure, and she partly dislocated her right shoulder. They're going to get her fixed up with a cast for her leg and something to keep her arm immobile, and then they want to keep her for observation because of the concussion."

"Okay. What do we do now?"

"You should go home." Jess put her hand on their shoulder. "Get some sleep, eat something. I'm going to put her on the waiting list for that home up in Ithaca, and when she gets out Timothy and I will take her home. After you've gotten some rest, you can look into talking to her landlord about getting her released from her lease. Then we can figure out how we're going to pay her new rent."

Wyatt wanted to insist that they needed to stay, but for what? There was nothing they could do here, their mother was being taken care of, Jess knew her way around this hospital a hundred times better than Wyatt did ... "Okay. But call me when she's ready to have visitors and when she's ready to be released, okay? I'll come and help you and Timothy move her into your house."

"Yeah." Jess hugged them again. "I'll definitely call you, okay?"

"Okay." Wyatt hugged her back, then went to collect their things.

"Don't worry," Timothy said as Wyatt pulled on their coat. "We'll call you if anything changes."

"Thanks." Wyatt gave Timothy a pat on the arm on their way to the door.

Wyatt let their forehead rest against the steering wheel for a moment before starting the car. Every part of their body hurt, and there was a dull pain behind their eyes. More than anything, Wyatt wanted to curl up with Grayson again and pretend like this had never happened. Their apartment was considerably closer to the hospital, though. Wyatt could just go there, put on fresh clothes, sleep for a couple hours, and then come back. Best to stay close in case something happened.

Mom's okay. Staying at the hospital for observation though, they texted Grayson. *Going back to my place for clean clothes.*

Grayson texted back almost immediately. *You want me to come over?*

No, sleep, Wyatt wrote. *I'll see you tomorrow.* They dropped their phone into the cup holder and pulled out of the lot.

The drive back to their apartment was a barely remembered blur of darkness, headlights, and snow. As soon as they got inside, they shed their coat and shoes and dropped back into bed.

Wyatt was shaking all over, heart hammering in their chest. Their breath came in ragged gasps, and sheer terror blinded them.

Get out, get out, get out, get out, get out.

The dimly lit room contracted, squeezing in on them. The shaking was getting worse, their chest squeezing tight as a fist with every breath. Their head swam, vision blurring from lack of oxygen. Wyatt forced themselves to roll over and fumbled with the bedside table until they managed to turn on the lamp. They sat up as soon as the light went on, scanning their bedroom as if expecting some kind of attack. Of course there was nothing there, no one waiting in the dark.

The T-shirt they'd worn to bed stuck to their back with sweat.

They scrubbed their hands across their face and drew their knees up to their chest. *Take one breath, then another, and another.* Leaning forward, Wyatt rocked back and forth until they stopped choking on nothing.

Fuck, it had been a long time since they'd woken up panicking like this. Wyatt reached for their phone, fumbled with their headphones, and hit one of the panic assistance apps.

Eventually, their breathing evened and the shaking lessened. Their skin prickled with cooled sweat, their head full of memories of fear and sadness.

Wyatt climbed out of bed and made for the bathroom, where they stripped out of their clothes and ran the shower lukewarm. Standing under the spray, they scrubbed themselves until their skin turned pink and blotchy.

God, what were they doing sleeping when there was so much that had to be dealt with?

They needed to go back to the hospital and see if Jess needed help getting her house ready for someone with mobility issues. They needed to contact their mother's landlord. They needed to go over their finances and see what could be changed to give them the extra money they'd need to make sure their mother was well taken care of. Maybe they'd have to move out of this apartment into a cheaper place. That would mean they'd need to contact their landlord and go apartment searching. Right now, Wyatt could think of a hundred ways each of these steps could go wrong. What if they never found the money to move their mother into a good assisted-living home, what then?

Wyatt's chest tightened again, their body going heavy with fear. They couldn't ... they couldn't ... Doubling over, Wyatt's stomach cramped and then flipped, and acid burned up their throat. They stumbled out of the shower and managed to make it to the toilet before they vomited.

There wasn't really anything left in their stomach to throw up, so Wyatt heaved up long ropes of yellow phlegm, then dry heaved until their stomach finally settled. Wyatt leaned their forehead against the edge of the bowl. Their legs ached where they'd fallen to the floor. They suspected they would find bruises later. Their throat burned, and their stomach was still cramping. Slowly, they became aware that they were soaking wet, naked, and increasingly cold.

After a few more moments, Wyatt pushed themselves up. Pain shot through their knees, making them wince and hiss. They limped to the shower, turned it off, and managed to get a towel out and wrap it around their waist.

Back in the bedroom, they sank onto the bed. What they really needed to do was get dressed, but

Wyatt didn't think they had enough energy to stand up again. Their whole body felt like it was made of lead, and more than anything they wanted to roll over and go back to sleep. Maybe things would be better next time they woke up if they went back to sleep for long enough. If they slept now, though, they might have whatever dream had woken them.

That fear alone was enough to keep them awake.

They laid unmoving, just staring at the ceiling for what seemed like hours. Finally, they forced themselves to reach for the bedside table and pick up their cell phone. Wyatt curled onto their side and unlocked it. There were no missed calls or text messages. The screen showed 4:13 a.m.

Their finger landed on Grayson's number and pressed CALL before they could talk themselves out of it.

It rang twice, then, "Hello?" Grayson's voice was a little slurred and fuzzy around the edges. "Wyatt, is that you? Has something happened? Is your Mom okay?"

Wyatt inhaled. There was no turning back now. "I ... I just ..." Their voice came out small and watery.

"Wyatt?" Grayson's voice had gone sharp. "Are you okay?"

Wyatt didn't know how to answer that. "No," they said finally.

There was a scuffling noise in the background, a bump as Grayson shifted the phone. "Tell me your address?"

It occurred to Wyatt that Grayson had never been to their apartment, and they were suddenly washed with shame because of it. Why hadn't they had Grayson over? They were being a shit partner, weren't they? They told Grayson their address, voice wobbling with sudden tears.

"Okay," Grayson said again. "Just hold tight, I'll be there in a few minutes."

The phone went dead against their ear, and Wyatt pulled it away to look down at it for a second. Then they went to find some clothes.

It wasn't even 5:00 a.m. yet. The sky was still a dark, dark gray outside the windows when their doorbell buzzed.

Standing on the stoop, Grayson looked rumpled but was fully dressed, right down to the sweater vest.

"Can I come in?" Grayson peered up at them.

"I'm sorry, of course you can." Wyatt stood back and ushered Grayson into their living room.

Wyatt realized once they had closed the door that their living room was a mess. There were books they needed to put away piled everywhere, papers from articles they'd printed off the Internet in order to better understand certain details of the cases they were working on scattered across the coffee table, couch, and floor. Both their sneakers and a pair of work shoes sat next to the couch, and their coat was on the floor where they'd dropped it the night before. Wyatt picked it up, trying to be as casual and inconspicuous as possible, and hung it by the door.

"Are you okay?" Grayson reached out toward Wyatt, hand hovering in the air between them like he was afraid that touching was the wrong thing to do.

Wyatt took two steps toward Grayson and burst into tears.

Grayson closed the distance between them. Wyatt bent forward, unable to stand upright anymore, and Grayson finally reached out, put his arms around Wyatt, guided them together so Wyatt's head could rest on Grayson's shoulder against the soft curve of his throat.

"I'm here. We're going to figure this out, yeah? You and your sister, me and you. We are going to get through this."

Wyatt couldn't answer between the sobs that twisted up from inside them with each heaving breath. They hung on Grayson as tightly as they could.

"If she died ..." Wyatt drew in a long, shaking breath. "All I ever think about is how much I wish things would go back to how they were before she got sick, how much her being sick hurts me." Wyatt sobbed again, and Grayson made soft noises.

"Hey." Grayson rubbed a soothing line up and down Wyatt's back. "It's obvious you love your mom."

"But I never stop and take the time to actually be with her." Wyatt could feel themselves shaking. "I worry about the money and resent how tired taking care of her makes me, how stressed I get over it, but I never think about how she must feel."

"I'm sure that's not actually true." Grayson's voice was soft and calm. "I think you're tired and stressed out now because someone you love is in the hospital. I also think caring for someone with Alzheimer's is difficult and draining. But I can't imagine you never show your mom that you care or never worry about her feelings. That's just not you."

Wyatt wished they could believe that, wished they saw themselves like Grayson did. All they could think about right now, though, were the times when even the idea of going to see their mother had turned their stomach with dread. They closed their eyes and pressed their face against Grayson's shoulder like it could block out the shame and the fear.

Grayson cradled the back of their head until Wyatt had cried all the tears they had.

"I'm sorry." They lifted their head and wiped their eyes and cheeks with one hand.

"It's all right." Grayson started trying to get his coat off without actually stepping back or letting go of Wyatt. Which was sweet but ended with him tangled up in coat, until Wyatt unlocked their fingers from Grayson's person and stepped away.

Wyatt folded themselves up on the couch while Grayson got his arms free of his coat, hung it up, and returned. He sat next to Wyatt, curled around them, resting his chin on Wyatt's shoulder.

Wyatt leaned into Grayson. Their body felt buzzing and light with nervous energy now that the wave of panic had somewhat subsided.

Wyatt's phone buzzed in their pocket, and they dug it out to see Jess had sent them a text: *Mom's awake.*

"I've got to go to the hospital." Wyatt pulled away and reached for the sneakers next to the couch. "My mom's up."

Grayson was frowning. "It's really early. I don't know if they'll let you in. Maybe you should just ..."

Hot rage filled Wyatt, just like that. It made tears prick at the corners of their eyes and their hands clench.

Grayson must have read it on their face, because he held up his hands in surrender. "I'm not trying to stop you from being with your mom. But you're exhausted, panicking, and it's only a little past the middle of the night."

There was a long, tense moment of silence.

"Here." Grayson stood as well. "Let me drive."

The anger drained away, leaving them feeling hollowed out and raw around the edges. It wasn't fair to get mad at Grayson of all people.

"Thanks." Wyatt looked down at the floor and concentrated on pulling on their shoes one at a time.

Grayson wrestled on his coat again, and they headed out into the early morning dark.

Wyatt stuck their hands in their pockets against the cold.

Their breath bloomed up between them, long tendrils of white under the streetlights.

The inside of Grayson's car was still a little warm from the trip over to Wyatt's apartment. The warmth made Wyatt feel guilty again, the emotion warring for space among all the others jumbled up inside them.

The two of them didn't talk. Wyatt kept their full concentration on their breathing, trying to stay calm and avoid another panic attack. They ran through every technique their therapist had showed them back when they'd gone to therapy. Beside them, Grayson was quiet and still in a way that made Wyatt think if they could just reach out, there would be a certain calm settled underneath Grayson's skin, in the curve of his wrist and the warmth of his hand against Wyatt's. Not like the stale, stifling heat coming from the car radiators, but sunlight and safety.

Wyatt kept their hands where they were, though, closed into loose fits on each knee, because if they reached out now, they wouldn't stop.

They were almost at the hospital.

When Grayson pulled into the emergency parking lot, the first thing Wyatt saw was Jess standing under one of the lights. Grayson parked the car but let it idle as Wyatt got out to trek across the stone and concrete.

"Did you get my texts?" Jess called when Wyatt was close enough to hear. "I was hoping you'd see them before you came over here again."

"I just read the first one." It seemed stupid now to have driven all the way here in what was for most people the dead of night without waiting for Jess to finish texting.

"Well, go home." She stuck her hands in her coat pockets, bouncing a little on her heels in an attempt to keep warm. "Mom's fine. You can see her tomorrow morning and talk. But right now, go get some sleep. That's what I'm going to do."

Wyatt nodded, a little bit numb.

"Is that your boyfriend in the car?"

They hesitated only for the barest moment. "Yeah."

"Well, tell him thanks for driving you." She smiled a little. "It was nice of him."

Wyatt looked back at Grayson still waiting for them to be done, hands cupped in front of his face to keep them warm.

"Yes, it was." It was really good not to be alone in this, to have Jess, Timothy, and Grayson.

"Get some sleep." She patted them on the shoulder. "I mean it, Wyatt, your body needs to rest. I'll see you tomorrow."

"Sure."

She turned back to the hospital.

"Back to your place?" Grayson asked when Wyatt climbed in next to him again.

"Yeah." Wyatt nodded. "Thank you. For driving, for dealing with me."

To Wyatt's surprise, Grayson smiled at that, like something about it was funny to him. "It's no problem."

He put the car into reverse, turning back the way they'd come.

Wyatt looked tired even asleep, sprawled across the couch. Grayson had been forced to wrestle them all the way on once Wyatt had fallen asleep, and to drape a blanket over them.

Maybe he should have gone home. Instead, he curled up in a chair next to the couch and closed his eyes. He dozed for a few hours until light creeping through the curtains woke him.

For a moment, he just sat there, letting last night come back to him. On the couch, Wyatt moved, pushing their face farther into the cushion. Grayson retrieved his cell phone off the coffee table and went to call the store.

They didn't really need him until the lunch rush anyway. Although calling in would probably mean his hours would be given to someone else. His boss could be a dick like that. He could double for the rest of the week if he had to, though, and just this once take it on the chin.

Wyatt was sitting up when Grayson came back into the living room. They looked rumpled and small wrapped up in the blankets, still in the clothes they'd been wearing since before Grayson had arrived.

"You okay?"

Wyatt rubbed one hand over their face. "I ... yeah, I think, better now I've slept."

"Good." Grayson sat at the edge of the couch next to Wyatt's legs.

"Thanks, by the way." Wyatt reached down and took Grayson's hand. "I was a little bit of an asshole last night."

"You were fine last night, considering what you're going through, and I didn't take it person-ally. Also,"—he pulled Wyatt's hand so it was pressed more securely against his thigh, cradled in his—"you don't have to keep thanking me for being here. I'm pretty sure as your boyfriend I'm supposed to be here."

For a split second, he was desperately afraid that he'd overstepped.

Then Wyatt sat up completely and kissed him; the press of lips, hands and blankets tangled between them. Grayson wanted to melt into Wyatt's warmth like he always did, to wrap himself up in it and stay there forever. Wyatt pulled away eventually, though.

"I got to go brush my teeth and change my clothes, I think." They scooted to the edge of the couch and stood.

"Okay." Grayson stayed where he was. "And when you're ready, let's track down a Dunkin Donuts or Starbucks before we go to the hospital."

Wyatt gave him a very small, exhausted smile. "That would be nice." They bent to kiss Grayson again, quickly this time before heading down the hall to the bathroom.

Grayson listened to the shower turn on and then reached for his phone to see where exactly they could pick up some coffee and breakfast on the way to the hospital.

Grayson's phone vibrated in his pocket as he unlocked the door to his house. His stomach dropped when he saw it was Bertha, but he answered it anyway.

"Hello."

"Hello." Bertha sounded as cheerful as usual on the other end. "How have you been lately?"

"I'm fine." Grayson closed the door behind him and kicked off his shoes while trying to free himself from his coat one-handed.

"Good, I'm glad to hear it, dear." And then she sighed. "So we had our monthly board meeting last night. And I'm afraid the consensus was we do not have the money to continuing allowing the historical society to be open into the next year."

"So what is this going to mean for me?" In the kitchen, Grayson leaned against a counter, one arm across him, holding the phone in the other hand.

"Well, your job will only be available until the end of the year." Bertha did sound apologetic. "I'm sorry, I really am, but there's just no way around it."

"Okay." Grayson rubbed his hand over his eyes. "Well, thank you for telling me."

"You should get the official email in the next few days. And take care of yourself, dear."

"Yes, you, too." He waited for her to hang up, then put the phone down on the coffee table.

So this was it. Come the end of the year, he'd be down one job. He'd need to find another one sometime soon, maybe another part-time one he could put on top of the deli job.

God, what a mess.

Right now, though, he needed to change out of his work clothes.

Once he'd showered and dressed, Grayson went into the kitchen to heat some water for tea.

When the water boiled, he sat down with a cup of tea and his laptop at the kitchen table.

He was already making one of the lowest student loan payments possible, the one that meant it would take him at least thirty years to pay it off. Would they even let him take a lower payment plan? Or was he going to have to cut money from somewhere else? Maybe he'd be able to cut a little from gas money and food.

Even setting aside how financially difficult this was going to make his life, losing this job would also mean he wouldn't be doing professional history anymore. When the year was up, he wouldn't be working in the field at all. The more years he spent outside the field, the harder it would be to get back into it. If he couldn't find another history job soon, he might never be able to get one at all. On top of that, Grayson had gotten his position at the Windsor Historical Society because he was local. To be competitive for work in another historical society or anything like that, he'd need a degree in library science specializing in archives.

He was going to be stuck behind the deli counter forever, and the two degrees he'd worked hard for would be meaningless.

Or he needed to stop thinking like that. Something would come up. He'd find his way back into the field.

It wasn't like leaving the historical society would stop him from doing research. He and Wyatt had the photographs to work on. It was more complex research than he'd done at the historical society anyway. It just didn't count on a curriculum vitae like the work at the historical society had.

Grayson took his cup of tea into the living room. He stopped at the little window, looking out at the trees in the back of the house. What would he do if he could no longer do historical work? What would it be like when that piece had finally gone from his life?

Outside, it was snowing, tiny flakes that melted into icy water as they touched the gray branches of the trees.

He turned from the window and went into his bedroom. Inside his desk was a pack of index cards left over from when he'd been a student. He turned on his desk lamp and put his cup of tea aside.

On each index card, he wrote a piece of the time-line they'd constructed for James and Liam. That they'd served together. Afterward, James had become a bookkeeper in Binghamton, and Liam had been involved in spiritualism in some way. They'd met up again when Liam had started the Binghamton spiri-tualist group? Or maybe before that? Had they kept in touch the whole time? Grayson had no idea. They did know that at some point after that, James and Liam had sat together for a portrait.

Not much of a timeline when you came right down to it, but now he had to figure out what to do with it.

He'd talked to Wyatt about making space. It was time to put his money where his mouth was. The reality of the situation was that he couldn't wait to do the research he wanted to do. There would probably be no job that paid him to do it—probably no job in his field, period—and no dissertation to research for.

If he wanted to do some creative queer history, it was now or never.

With the timeline so spotty, obviously it would take some creative interpretation to make this into anything useful. Grayson dragged a box of academic books out of his closet and started going through them, looking for anything that might be helpful. Luckily for them, the ones he'd kept were mostly on queer history. Most of them he'd gotten while writing his thesis, written by historians he admired on topics he'd found meaningful or important.

He hauled out Foucault, Butler, and Chauncey, not sure any of them would help him. Might as well read them over again and find out, though. At the bottom of the box was a copy of Avery Gordon's *Ghostly Matters*, so he picked that one up, too, and carried his armful to the bed, where he dumped it. He sat beside the pile of books with his tea and started going through them, jotting notes and quotes down on the index cards.

There wasn't a whole lot that was directly applicable to what Grayson wanted to do. Even so, if anything sparked an idea, he noted it. Hopefully some of this would be helpful later on.

Next to him on the bed, his phone vibrated with a text from Wyatt.

Can I come over?

Of course, he texted back. *I'll make dinner.* Although now that he thought about it, he had no idea what kind of ingredients he had.

On my way.

Grayson tucked the phone into his pocket and went to search through the refrigerator and cupboards for dinner.

There was a box of spaghetti and a jar of tomato sauce, so he put both on the counter. When Wyatt arrived, he'd ask if spaghetti was okay, and if not, they could maybe find something else.

By the time he heard tires on the driveway, Grayson had moved all his research into the living room along with his index cards and computer.

"Hey," Wyatt said when Grayson opened the door.

"Hey. How's your mom doing?" He stepped back to let Wyatt in.

"Settling in at Jess's okay." Wyatt still looked exhausted, too pale, with dark circles under their eyes. They carried a bottle of wine in one hand but hesitated when they stepped into the house, looking down at Grayson.

"What?" Grayson tipped his head up to look back, and Wyatt bent and kissed him on the lips. It was just a soft brush, and then they were straightening up again.

"I missed you." Grayson blinked.

"I missed you, too."

"I brought wine." Wyatt held up the bottle. "From Jess for the other night at the hospital. Should I put it in the kitchen?"

"That would be great." Grayson followed them into the kitchen. "And tell Jess thanks next time you see her."

"I will." Wyatt put the wine on the counter. They stepped into the living room and surveyed the books and index cards spread across the coffee table and sofa. "What have you been up to in here?"

"I—" He didn't really know what to say that wouldn't sound stupid or pathetic. *I want to do something I'm good at, something.* It sounded ... "Just research," he said. "Thought, you know, I'd do it right."

Wyatt seemed to take the statement at face value. They nodded and picked up Grayson's copy of *Bodies That Matter*, frowning at the page it was open to.

"I was hoping to write something," Grayson said. "Something about the photographs, like a paper or an article." He trailed off, but Wyatt was nodding.

"Sounds like a good idea," Wyatt said, to Grayson's relief. "Can I help?"

"Of course you can." Grayson sat on the couch, and Wyatt sat beside him, a small stack of books between them. "I'm just brainstorming right now and writing anything I think will be useful down on the index cards."

"Like what kind of ideas?" Wyatt bent forward to read the index cards.

"I've been doing a lot of thinking about what you've said about the photographs being almost candid or having that feeling." Grayson took a breath. "And thinking about the nature of photographs as historical sources is all about the details. There's a bigger narrative around the photograph and then what the photograph actually tells us, a smaller reading. So in this case, the bigger picture being the possibility of a queer and trans past, but the smaller one being about these people in this one moment of their lives."

Wyatt was nodding, slow and thoughtful, turning over the cards where Grayson had written little bits and pieces of theory. "We can talk about what's obscured and what isn't, what's hidden and what's not," they said. "Feeding into the bigger picture, but also taking the time to celebrate the specific case of this moment, these two people, these photographs for being what they are."

"Exactly." Grayson picked up one of the books on the coffee table. "But for right now, I'm going through books looking for anything useful."

"Let me help." Wyatt settled into the couch.

By the time the sky had darkened outside the windows, Grayson was sitting on the floor, back against the couch, laptop perched on the coffee table along with a stack of index cards. Wyatt was sprawled behind him, immersed in George Chauncey's *Gay New York*.

"You want to think about what we're going to eat?" Grayson turned so he could look up at Wyatt.

"I didn't know any of this," Wyatt said, more to the book than Grayson. "Why didn't I know any of this?

Why isn't this covered in high school, or at the very least in US history?"

"Politics."

Wyatt looked down at him, and Grayson shrugged. "What gets taught at anything lower than a three-hundred-level college course is very political. You were never taught queer history because there are people with a vested interest in your not learning queer history. But the same thing can be said for race history—of all sorts—and most gender history, too, not to mention disability history. We don't learn it, not because historians don't study it but because the people who make the decision what goes into history textbooks aren't fans. Come on." He patted Wyatt's leg before standing. "Let's make dinner."

They made spaghetti and ate at Grayson's kitchen table with the wine Wyatt had brought. When they were done, they cleaned up the kitchen before ending up back on the couch.

Wyatt had poured them both a glass of wine and held theirs between their hands for a moment before they retrieved *Gay New York* and started to read.

By the time he'd finished his glass of wine, Grayson had the sinking feeling they were going to have to come up with their own theory and methodology for this. Which sucked, because usually historical research did not require you to come up with methodology, theory, *and* the actual research at the same time.

Grayson sat back and rubbed his eyes.

"Hey." Wyatt's hand touched the back of his neck, and Grayson turned to look up at them.

"Hey, yourself."

"You look tired." Wyatt's fingers found where the muscles were tightest and rubbed in little circles there.

"I'm just hoping we can do this." Grayson turned even farther so he could kiss Wyatt. Their fingers touched Grayson's hair and skimmed across the side of his face.

Grayson pulled away finally and climbed onto the couch, pushing books out of the way. He leaned into Wyatt and kissed them again.

Wyatt made a *hmph* noise as Grayson leaned his full weight against them, but they wrapped their arms around Grayson and pulled him close.

It was nice, snuggled up together. But Wyatt's hipbone was grinding into his thigh. He wiggled around until it wasn't, making Wyatt break the kiss with a pained grunt.

"Stop moving."

"I'm sorry, your hip was jabbing me." Grayson shifted again, making Wyatt gasp.

"You're too heavy on top of me. Let's try it the other way."

Grayson sighed and then stood up, and Wyatt pushed themselves up too. They readjusted on the couch with Grayson against one arm and Wyatt half leaning against him. It was a little bit cramped, the angle a little awkward, but then Wyatt leaned in and kissed Grayson again, all sweet warmth and tasting of wine, and it didn't matter at all.

CHAPTER 12

The snow fell deep enough to soak the landscape in white and gray. Grayson had bought a couple strings of Christmas lights from the dollar store and strung them around the edges of the windows. He'd brought home a little potted pine tree that no one had chosen at the store, put it on the kitchen table, and decorated it with tiny ornaments cut out of wrapping paper.

He'd had an interview at Maines, the restaurant supply store in town. The young woman who'd interviewed him had been impressed with his years of work at Schroder's. He'd almost certainly get the job, she said, especially if he was willing to pick up extra hours over the holidays.

For Grayson, it would be a way to make up the money he'd lose when the historical society let him go at the end of the year.

When he pulled into his driveway several days later, Wyatt was already there, leaning against their car, arms folded over their chest.

The two of them entered the house together and did a little dance around each other as they both tried to take their coats and boots off at the same time.

Grayson was hyper-aware that he still wore his work uniform and smelled like sweat and the inside of a deli case. Wyatt, on the other hand, was dressed in a pleated wool skirt, black tights with a little bit of a lace pattern, and a button-up blouse and cardigan. Grayson wanted to touch Wyatt, hug and kiss them, but he also didn't want to get near their beautiful clothes without taking a shower first.

Wyatt bent and kissed Grayson anyway, sweaty clothes and all, and Grayson was so caught by it he kissed back, letting one hand come up to cup Wyatt's cheek.

"Jess asked about you, you know," Wyatt said when their lips parted. Wyatt hadn't moved back yet. They stood much closer than Grayson could believe anyone would want to, considering his preshowered state. "Asked if I was going to see my boyfriend today."

Grayson swallowed, his throat dry. "Oh, yeah? What did you tell her?"

Wyatt was smiling now. "I said yes, yes I was."

"Oh?" Grayson got out, before Wyatt kissed him again, and this time Grayson didn't care—he put his arms around Wyatt's neck and pulled them close.

The two of them both leaned back a little, and Grayson took Wyatt in. "You look beautiful today."

Wyatt laughed against Grayson's neck. "You like it?"

"I do." Grayson drew them a little closer, just to prove it. "You should do this more often."

"Wear a skirt?"

Grayson smiled. "Be yourself."

Wyatt's arms tightened around Grayson, and they clung to him, face pressed into Grayson's neck.

For a few moments, Grayson held the two of them up there in his hallway.

Then Wyatt's arms loosened, and they pulled back enough to meet Grayson's eyes. "Thank you."

"Don't thank me." Grayson kissed them again. "I want you to be happy and feel safe with me. I'm glad that you do."

"I do." Wyatt cupped his cheek, kissed Grayson briefly, just a quick brush of lips.

Grayson wanted to kiss them again. He wanted to strip them out of that cardigan and blouse and push his hands up under the skirt. They were still in the hall, though, surrounded by boots and melting snow, with a strong draft coming from the door. Plus, he smelled like the backroom of a deli.

"I, uh, just got back from work." Grayson drew away from Wyatt. "And I should probably shower."

Wyatt blinked at him. "Sure. I'll wait in the living room."

"Or anywhere. Wherever you want, make yourself comfortable." Grayson gave them a quick smile and then darted off toward his bedroom and the bathroom.

He tried to be as fast as possible, picking out his clothes, showering, and dressing.

Wyatt was sitting on the couch when Grayson got back to the living room, finger combing his wet hair as he walked.

"I have something for you." Wyatt's hands were balled in their lap. They looked nervous.

"What?"

"Just hear me out before you get angry," Wyatt said, which didn't make Grayson feel any better.

"What?" His nerves had started to creep into his voice.

"Here." Wyatt picked up a folded piece of paper from the coffee table. They fiddled with it for a moment before handing to Grayson.

Grayson unfolded it to find it wasn't a piece of paper at all but a check, made out to him for seventy-five dollars.

"Money's going to get tight soon." Wyatt wasn't looking at him now. "When I start contributing to getting my Mom into a good place. But I figured while I still had it ..."

They trailed off, and Grayson held out the check. "What is this for?"

"Syracuse University has one of the best programs in library information science in the country." Wyatt finally looked at Grayson. "And it's close, close enough to commute or do online after the first year. With a master's in history and a master's in library science, you could work anywhere, for any university, in an archive or special collection. You could work, and you could do history. Some places consider you a faculty member, you know, working as an archivist. They don't require the GREs if you already have a master's degree, so no worries about that." Wyatt stopped. They stared at each other. Wyatt licked their lips and went on. "Seventy-five dollars is the application fee, so you don't have to worry about that either."

"I can't—" Grayson extended the check toward Wyatt, and Wyatt held up their hand.

"Please, keep it, and at least think about applying, okay? I know it's not as good as a PhD, but it's pretty close, right? And it's only three or four semesters and an internship. They fund their students, they offer them jobs, too, working in the archives, special collections, book restoration unit, audio archives—all on campus. You could quit the job you have now. You could do what you've always wanted."

Grayson's fingers closed around the check. He rested his hand in his lap. Could he go back to school and become an archivist? He could work at a historical society again, maybe a museum or, best of all, a college or university. Paying for two years sounded so much more doable and realistic than the five minimum for a PhD. He could do research and writing. He could do history again.

"Yeah, it might work." He looked up at Wyatt. "Thank you."

Wyatt leaned forward and kissed him. Grayson kissed them back, holding onto Wyatt, arms around them. Everything in Grayson wanted to be closer, to touch Wyatt, to keep on touching them.

Wyatt wrapped their arms around Grayson's waist and pulled him half into their lap. Grayson started laughing, breaking the kiss, and sat back on his heels.

"Come on." He stood and held out his hand to Wyatt. "Let's go find a bed to do this on."

Grayson's bedroom was dark when they stumbled into it, the light off and curtains closed. Grayson didn't really care. He used his hands to map the lines of Wyatt's body.

Wyatt kissed him again as Grayson fumbled with Wyatt's cardigan, trying to push it off.

"Here." Wyatt pushed Grayson's hands away and stripped off the cardigan and shirt under it themselves.

Grayson's hands started at the waistband of the skirt, trailing up across Wyatt's chest. He could feel Wyatt's ribs, the way they breathed, and as his hands traveled up, Wyatt's heartbeat. Grayson kissed the path his hands had traveled and Wyatt sighed, hand against Grayson's back and then up to cup the back of his head.

Wyatt's fingers tightened for a moment in Grayson's hair. Grayson looked up at that, and Wyatt kissed him again on the lips.

Grayson pulled his sweater vest off when they parted, unbuttoned his shirt, pushing it off and pulling his binder over his head.

Wearing only his slacks, he pulled Wyatt to the bed and pushed them down. He stretched himself over Wyatt, so that his hips pressed between Wyatt's legs and their chests touched.

Wyatt's fingers traced up Grayson's arms, followed the path of his clavicle.

"Can I?" they said, voice soft, fingers touching the skin between Grayson's collar and breasts.

"Yes." Grayson's voice trembled, and Wyatt's hand skimmed down to touch just the top, fragile skin with stretch marks like rivers running down the sides of each breast. Wyatt's fingers ran with the flow of them down to each pink nipple. Grayson's fingers tightened around Wyatt's upper arms, and he rocked his hips against Wyatt's. He pulled away and sat up enough to try to wrestle off his pants. Wyatt unzipped their skirt.

They pushed close again when their clothes were off. Wyatt laughed, a little breathless. "Come here." They held out their arms, and Grayson almost fell on them, leaning into the embrace with enough enthusiasm to knock the breath out of Wyatt.

Grayson kissed them, quick and sloppy, before sliding down against Wyatt's body.

He stopped where he could rest his head against Wyatt's chest. Wyatt pushed between Grayson's thighs. They thrust their hips, and Grayson let his legs press closed. Gently—he didn't want to hurt Wyatt, who had their hands on Grayson's hips now. Wyatt's hips moved a little erratically against Grayson. Grayson's own hips began to move, too, seeking friction.

It was a little bit awkward the way their bodies moved against each other. Wyatt's body warm against his, their hips, thighs, and soft skin rubbing against him, made Grayson gasp and clutch at Wyatt. He thrust harder as Wyatt rubbed against him with more urgency.

The two of them were out of sync again; the push and pull of them moving against each other didn't seem to have any rhythm to it.

It didn't matter.

Wyatt was all silken skin, flushed hot against Grayson's body, their mouth open pressed against Grayson's neck. Their fingers gripped at Grayson's body hard enough to bruise, and Grayson wanted that, wanted to feel the ghost of this on him for days.

Wyatt panted, "Please, please, please." Soft and low, until Grayson kissed them, took the words out of their mouth into his own, swallowed them whole. Then Wyatt worked a hand between them and Grayson couldn't not pull back gasping, pushing himself into Wyatt's hand.

"Going to take care of you." Wyatt stroked him in a way that made everything turn into liquid need, all singing through him saying, *Yes, there, please.*

"Fuck," was the only thing Grayson got out, though, as his body tightened and then just fell—or maybe he jumped.

Their bodies were still pressed together when Grayson came back to himself. Wyatt was still all sweetness and desperation. Grayson wanted to taste it, wanted nothing more than to touch Wyatt forever. His hands moved, cupping, encouraging, stroking, pressing until Wyatt was a writhing, gasping, wide-eyed mess from it. So beautiful, Grayson thought. So, so beautiful, and just for him. Wyatt's hands tangled in his, and then Wyatt tensed, coming in a long, fluid shudder.

For a few moments, Grayson stayed where he was, lying across Wyatt's body. Then he rolled over so he could lie against the cool bedcovers. "If you want to take a shower, go ahead."

"I don't suppose your shower is big enough for both of us."

They sounded hopeful, and Grayson laughed. "It's going to be barely big enough for just you."

"Ah, well." Wyatt rolled onto their stomach and leaned over to give Grayson a kiss. "Next time, we'll have to do this at my apartment, where I have a tub we can both fit into."

Grayson curled up on the bed and listened to the sounds of Wyatt moving across the room and into the bathroom. The pipes creaked as Wyatt turned on the water.

He closed his eyes and let his breathing even out.

They were going to be okay.

CHAPTER 13

Wyatt sat at their dining room table, laptop open in front of them. On the screen was a digital copy of the second photograph, and next to the computer was the original.

The second photograph did show Liam holding a cigarette in one hand, as they had suspected, and James did look perilously close to cracking a smile, caught in this moment with Liam, their hands together.

Thomas had found the original in the depths of an archive somewhere, Grayson had said. Unearthed by a friend of a friend who'd had to dig for it, unlabeled and undated. Only their military rank and the long, winding trail of their pay records had made them possible to find.

"Unknown soldiers," the photograph had been labeled before Grayson and Wyatt found it.

Wyatt stared at them, Liam's face guarded as ever, his eyes in this light unreadable. James, for all that he seemed to be filled with joy here, rather than nervous energy, remained serious and stern.

Still secrets there, Wyatt thought, touching their fingers to the scene. *Still not giving much away.*

Then Wyatt thought about Grayson, the weight of Grayson's hand in theirs, the way he curled himself against Wyatt when they slept, the smell of his hair and the feel of his hands against the nape of Wyatt's neck. They thought about the way Grayson laughed early in the morning, when there was still sleep in his voice.

There were things they kept secret even now. Not because they were ashamed, but because some things were too precious to share. Wyatt thought there was a difference there. Or maybe the kinds of secrets they kept were too entwined to be so easily separated.

They looked down at the photograph again. In the beginning, they had thought James and Liam were hiding. Now they weren't so sure.

The language of analyzing, of reading and uncovering, was interesting to Wyatt, but it was ultimately Grayson's language.

What Wyatt wanted was to witness these moments, the lives of these two people: who they had been and who they were.

To witness something was to give it a life of its own outside of yourself. Wyatt felt that was the most fitting for speaking of the past.

The past existed, remembered or not, acknowledged or not. Because at the end of the day, it was the lived experience of people whose lives and personhood were not easily erased.

Even without Wyatt's dreaming and wondering, without Grayson's theories and writing, James and Liam had lived and loved. They might lay forgotten somewhere, unnoticed, lost—but that didn't stop them from being real. It didn't stop everything in their lives from having happened.

History was pieces of real experience, people who'd lived and died and left things behind.

Like a photograph, tucked into an envelope and hidden away.

Wyatt touched their faces. "You existed and you still exist. I know it, and I see you."

Then they pulled on their coat and went to find Grayson.

Grayson brought home a small box of stuff from the historical society. It had all the things he'd taken into the office over the years he'd worked there, things that didn't belong to the historical society.

One night, he sat at the kitchen table with a cup of tea and went through the box.

There were papers mixed together with paper clips, staples, rubber bands, and pieces of string Grayson didn't even know why he had.

Grayson sorted out the papers, smoothing each one as he did. There were some notes he'd forgotten he'd made about the photograph.

Shirley did work on race for this time period, didn't she? Although he thought she focused on New York City. He fetched his computer anyway and sent an email off. Not for the first time, he wished he had access to an academic library and the ability to inter-library loan. There was probably stuff out there they were completely missing without access to journal databases.

The reason for doing this still nagged at him. Without proper access to resources, without much hope of publishing, of writing anything substantive, what were they building together, Wyatt and him?

He left the table piled with papers and took his cup to the sink before heading out the front door.

The sky was still gray, not quite dark as Grayson turned toward the woods.

Beyond the woods was the field where he and Wyatt had walked, and beyond that more woods.

The snow wasn't thick under the trees. There was just a light dusting except where a little extra had blown into small dunes that feathered out toward each tree trunk.

In the forest between the trees was a pile of stones partly covered by the snow. Grayson moved toward it, and it wasn't until he was nearly on top of it that he realized it was part of a low stone wall that had half collapsed. He stood there, hands in pockets, looking down at it.

When he'd been a child, his grandmother had lived out in this area, and in the summer his whole family would pack up and move into her rundown farmhouse. In the woods behind her house was a small creek that he and Steve had loved to play in, the water coming up to their knees in some places.

Beyond the creek, farther into the woods, was a hole in the ground. His father had told him it was an old slate quarry and they shouldn't go near it, but of course they had. Grayson could still remember the time they'd climbed down to the bottom of the hole, standing and looking up at the walls around them. It was like standing in an amphitheater of black stone. The experience had made his hands shake with a mixture of fear and excitement. He'd pressed himself close to Steve, because those were the days when Steve had been his big brother, who, Grayson believed, would never let him get hurt.

Also in the woods were stone fences, built before the quarries. When the first white settlers had moved into the region, they'd built houses and farms, land marked off by fences made out of slate.

When the houses were gone—the farms, the animals, the people, even their graves gone into the ground—the fences remained.

In this woods once, when the trees had been young and even before, someone had made a home, farmed the hard, rocky land, and built a fence.

Grayson stared at the fence where the stones had fallen down, half covered with snow and dried leaves. The part of it that still stood was coated in mosses, small climbing plants now brown, and a thick layer of pine needles.

He reached down and put one hand on the cold stone of the fence.

There was an image that had stayed with him since his first year of graduate school. Walter Benjamin had written that history was a catastrophe piling wreckage at the feet of an angel, arms outstretched but unable to hold it back.

Grayson had long imagined history like that.

Those we most needed to remember passed out of time. History enabled and forgot and destroyed, and so often there was just nothing left behind. Worse than wreckage is absence.

Some parts of our past, Avery Gordon said in her book about haunting and the social imagination, are lost so completely that only ghosts remain.

In that way, we are linked to a past we don't or can't remember.

What happens when your history has been destroyed, or forgotten, or lost?

Who are you when you can't look behind you and say, *There were people like me, who lived full lives, did amazing things and were happy?*

Who are you then?

His hand was cold, chilled to the point where he could barely feel his fingers. Grayson pulled it away from the stones and tucked it back into his pocket.

It was almost dark, so he turned back to the house.

When he got closer, he could see Wyatt's car parked in the driveway. As he watched, Wyatt opened the door and climbed out.

Grayson picked up his pace.

"Hey," Wyatt said when they were close, smiling down at Grayson, and pulled him into a hug.

"Come on." Grayson drew away. "Let's go inside."

Inside, Grayson put on a kettle for tea. It was Wyatt who pressed him back against the counter and kissed him. Wyatt's lips were still cold, as was their nose where it bumped against Grayson's. Wyatt's hands snuck under Grayson's sweater, traced Grayson's hips, following along the top of his belt. Grayson leaned in close again. Wyatt kissed them back with everything he had.

"What were you doing out there in the woods?"

"Thinking about history." Grayson looked up at them. "I was thinking about the way that we lose people—or lose track of people, I guess. The way the past swallows them up and there's only shadows left, but I think ..." He took Wyatt's hand in his. "I don't know, maybe we can make it different, even just a little bit. Everyone always talks about making the future, but maybe we can make the past instead."

And maybe that was a good enough reason to do this. Maybe it didn't have to be any more complicated than that.

For a long moment, they just watched each other. Then Wyatt bent and brushed a kiss across Grayson's lips. When they straightened back up, they were smiling. "Maybe we can. Maybe we will."

In answer, Grayson took their hand in his and led them farther into the house.

AUTHOR'S ACKNOWLEDGMENTS

There are so many people who had a hand in this book.

I need to thank Alexis Hall for his encouragement and support during the writing and editing process.

Also thanks to Ruthie Knox and Mary Ann Rivers for working really closely with me throughout.

I have had the pleasure and privilege to work with many great historians, but I need to mention two:

Peter Cline, who first introduced me to queer history and thought I had important things to say about it. I like to think he would have found this book and his hand in it delightful.

And Shirley Lim, who pushed me to see photographs as the key to unlocking a queer history of working-class people in the United States.

ABOUT THE AUTHOR

EE Ottoman grew up surrounded by the farmlands and forests of Upstate New York. They started writing as soon as they learned how and have yet to stop. Ottoman attended Earlham College and graduated with a degree in history before going on to receive a graduate degree in history as well. These days, they divide their time between history, writing, and book preservation.

Ottoman is also a queer, disabled, trans man whose pronouns are they/them/their or he/him/his. Mostly, though, they are a person who is passionate about history, stories, and the spaces between the two.

CREDITS

Author	EE Ottoman
First Readers	Alison Evans and Marie Hogebrandt
Series Editor	Alexis Hall
Copyeditor	Ruthie Knox
Cover Photograph	Nathan Pearce
Cover Design	Ranita Haanen
Interior Design	Medlar Publishing Inc